MORE MYSTERIES FROM THE BERKLEY PUBLISHING GROUP . . .

CAT CALIBAN MYSTERIES: She was married for thirty-eight years. Raised three kids. Compared to that, tracking down killers is easy . . .

by D. B. Borton

ONE FOR THE MONEY	TWO POINTS FOR MURDER
THREE IS A CROWD	FOUR ELEMENTS OF MURDER
FIVE ALARM FIRE	SIX FEET UNDER

ELENA JARVIS MYSTERIES: There are some pretty bizarre crimes deep in the heart of Texas—and a pretty gutsy police detective who rounds up the unusual suspects . . .

by Nancy Herndon

ACID BATH	WIDOWS' WATCH
HUNTING GAME	LETHAL STATUES

FREDDIE O'NEAL, P.I., MYSTERIES: You can bet that this appealing Reno private investigator will get her man . . . "A winner." —Linda Grant

by Catherine Dain

LAY IT ON THE LINE	SING A SONG OF DEATH
WALK A CROOKED MILE	LAMENT FOR A DEAD COWBOY
BET AGAINST THE HOUSE	THE LUCK OF THE DRAW
DEAD MAN'S HAND	

BENNI HARPER MYSTERIES: Meet Benni Harper—a quilter and folk-art expert with an eye for murderous designs . . .

by Earlene Fowler

FOOL'S PUZZLE	IRISH CHAIN
KANSAS TROUBLES	GOOSE IN THE POND

HANNAH BARLOW MYSTERIES: For ex-cop and law student Hannah Barlow, justice isn't just a word in a textbook. Sometimes, it's a matter of life and death . . .

by Carroll Lachnit

MURDER IN BRIEF	A BLESSED DEATH

DEAD MAN'S HAND

Catherine Dain

BERKLEY PRIME CRIME, NEW YORK

DEAD MAN'S HAND

A Berkley Prime Crime Book / published by arrangement with the author

PRINTING HISTORY
Berkley Prime Crime edition / April 1997

The Putnam Berkley World Wide Web site address is
http://www.berkley.com/berkley

ISBN: 0-425-15760-1

Berkley Prime Crime Books are published by The Berkley Publishing Group, 200 Madison Avenue, New York, NY 10016.
The name BERKLEY PRIME CRIME and the BERKLEY PRIME CRIME design are trademarks belonging to Berkley Publishing Corporation.

PRINTED IN THE UNITED STATES OF AMERICA

10 9 8 7 6 5 4 3 2 1

DEAD MAN'S HAND

Chapter

1

"I DON'T GET along with my own mother. What the hell makes you think I can get along with yours?"

"Reciprocity, of course. I like your mother a lot."

I was going to point out that the reciprocity of warmth that my friend Curtis and my mother Ramona felt for each other might not be mirrored by a Reno private eye and a Richmond socialite, when an elf smacked my knee.

My evil eye froze him in his tracks until his mother grabbed him. She glared at me for scaring the kid. I glared right back.

Bah, humbug.

With seven shopping days to go before Christmas, the mall was a mass of shoulder-to-shoulder wool starting to steam from the stress sweat working its way to the surface. Large packages moving into overheated stores bumped larger ones coming out. Something that sounded like "Trisha Yearwood Does Christmas" was coming over the loudspeakers, and the year-round smell of cinnamon from the fast-food bakery was in the air. Despite bright red and green decorations and lots of jingling bells, nobody looked any happier than I felt.

Actually, I was happy about a lot of things. Curtis Breckinridge, for one. Three months of fairly serious stuff, and I hadn't had an urge to head for the hills. My friend Sandra liked him almost as much as my mother did. Deke, my other friend, had grudgingly accepted him. My cats ignored him.

His colleagues at the university, especially the few who had become friends during the past year, his first in Reno, thought I was an interesting break from the academic circle.

But his mother was flying out for Christmas.

Christmas was thus primed to be the first serious test of our relationship. Maybe the second, if you count a murder at the university that ended badly for all concerned. And we had survived that. But it hadn't hit close to home in the same way.

The Tolstoy line about unhappy families all being different is crap. There are only two kinds of unhappy families—the ones who forget their differences long enough to celebrate the holidays and the ones who use the holidays as an opportunity to inflict maximum damage on whoever shows up. Curtis came from the first kind. I came from the second. Ramona and I were both doing our best, but it was too late for some things to change.

Curtis had started looking forward to Thanksgiving right after Halloween, just as I had started looking forward to January second.

And his mother was flying out for Christmas.

I glanced around the mall hoping I'd find a time warp to next year. I couldn't even see an exit. The stores were all at angles to one another, displays running together like a house of mirrors.

I did see two teenaged boys who seemed to be staring at

us through the crowd. When I caught the glance of the taller of the two, he grabbed his buddy's arm and pulled him toward the Nature's Wonders doorway.

"How much more do you need to buy?" I asked Curtis.

My shopping had been easily done, except for whatever I was going to give Curtis. I hadn't figured that out yet. I had tried to pick out a black leather purse for Ramona, hoping she would trash the one with the sequined rose. Curtis had talked me into buying her a fake leopard-print vest instead. "She may not be the mother you want, but she's the one you've got," was what he had said. He was right. And he didn't argue with a navy blue sweater for Al, her husband.

Sandra and I would exchange greetings of some sort. Deke didn't want to give Christmas presents any more attention than I did. So that was my Christmas shopping.

Curtis had already shipped packages to two siblings and their families, presented gifts to the department secretaries, and today had bought earrings, cologne, and a cowboy hat for his mother. The earrings were small sapphire studs in gold filigree. Sapphires were his mother's birthstone. I couldn't imagine either giving or receiving a Christmas gift that expensive.

"We can leave if you like," he replied.

"I do like, but I can stand it if you need more time."

"No, that's all right. We should probably think about dinner anyway."

"Great idea. There's a Mexican place right up the street."

"There's a Mexican place here in the mall, if that's what you want."

"I need to get out of the mall. My claustrophobia is beginning to act up."

"Okay. Do you mind dropping the packages off at my place first?"

"You could lock them in the trunk."

"I could, but I'd rather lock them in the apartment."

I wanted to tell Curtis that he'd lived too long in Southern California, but truthfully, he was right. Reno had changed over the years, becoming less Western and more urban, with bigger neighborhoods but fewer neighbors, to the point where it was reminding me more and more of the old Las Vegas, before that city morphed into Disneyland's evil twin.

Maintaining law and order in Reno was never as easy as people like to believe. Any casual reading of history is a reminder that the good old days were raw and uncivilized. Still, crime seemed to become more prevalent as the population exploded and the income polarization that had always characterized the city became more pronounced. The packages would be safer in his deadbolted apartment, in his security building, than in the trunk of his car.

"No problem" was all I said.

He tacked to his left toward a hole between stores, an aisle that I hoped might lead to the parking lot, but which only took us to the central atrium.

"How do you know where you're going?" I asked.

"It's a mall. If you know one mall, you know them all. Replace Macy's with Nordstrom's, and they're all the same. Disney, Gap, Limited, Eddie Bauer's, and a food court. San Fernando Valley yuppies buy their boot-cut jeans from the same Western wear chain you do. You'd know where you're going if they'd had malls in Reno when you were a kid."

"There are still two local Western wear stores. And I still buy from them."

He glanced at me, amused, and kept moving through the crowd. He was right, though. They didn't have malls in Reno when I was a kid, or at least not big enclosed ones like this. Malls with chain stores were another one of the changes I didn't like much.

As we excused ourselves through the line waiting for a

cottony Santa, I spotted the runaway elf. I resisted the urge to smack him with my packages, but only because I saw the Exit sign.

The sun sets early in late December, and the sky had turned black in the short while we had been inside. So I didn't spot the two teenagers again until we were well out of the mall and hurrying across the parking lot toward Curtis's Volvo.

And I didn't spot the gun until it was pointed at Curtis's chest.

"The small package," the kid said. The gun looked like a nine millimeter, something that needed two shaky hands to hold it up. The teenager's lips were trembling, too. And his wide, dark eyes appeared on the edge of tears. "The one in your pocket. And your wallet."

The kid with the quivering gun was the taller of the two. His short partner was standing off to the side, nervously watching for anyone who might interfere. Both were dark-haired and olive-skinned, dressed in Army surplus jackets over plaid shirts and jeans. They could have been brothers.

"Oh, hell," Curtis sighed. "Seventeen years in Los Angeles without a mugging. Now this."

"Just give him what he wants. I'm sorry. I saw them earlier, and I should have known something was wrong."

"Hurry up!" the anxious watcher called. He twitched for a second, then slipped between two diagonally parked cars and ran up the next aisle toward the street.

I turned to see who was coming. Two heavyset men in cowboy hats and down jackets were heading in our direction, loaded down with packages. I think Curtis might have turned, too. Something must have freaked the kid. Or maybe his trigger finger just had an uncontrollable spasm. I don't know. I didn't see the shot.

I heard it, and I dropped to my knees and slipped my gun

out of my boot without thinking. When I was hit by a falling package and realized that Curtis had crumpled to the ground beside me, I aimed and fired without thinking.

By the time the two men reached us, I was holding onto Curtis and sobbing, trying to stop his chest from bleeding, and the teenaged boy with the gun wasn't moving.

Chapter
2

I RODE WITH Curtis in the ambulance to the Washoe Medical Trauma Center.

One of the cowboys had stayed with me while the other found a security guard who called the paramedics. The security guard had wanted me to wait for the police, but when I gave him my gun and my business card, he let me go. He also offered to keep our packages. I managed to choke out a thank you.

The paramedics hooked Curtis to a monitor and slapped an oxygen mask on his face, then checked to make sure that the blood on my face and hands and clothes wasn't my own. A young man who looked so much like the one I had just shot that I couldn't stop shaking as he touched me cleaned as much of the blood off me as he could. I watched the shaky red line that meant Curtis's heart was still beating.

The kid on the pavement didn't go with us.

I hadn't ever expected to kill anybody with the All American .22 that I carried in my boot. I carried it as much for the surprise factor as anything else. Doing any real damage with a .22 depends on luck. If the teenager had had any, the bullet would have grazed his cheek and chased him off. But the bullet had hit him squarely, right in front of his ear, at an upward angle. I couldn't have counted on doing that even if I'd wanted to kill him. The gun is too small to be that accurate.

I had seen violent death before—not often enough to be comfortable with it—but I had never directly caused it. I had thought about causing it, abstractly at the gun range, when I fired at the target outline of a human being, and more concretely after I once shot and wounded a man who threatened my life. I knew I could shoot to kill if I had to. I never really believed that I would have to.

I hadn't even believed it this time.

I wasn't certain I believed it yet.

The paramedics who had cleaned my face assured me that Curtis's vital signs were strong. That didn't keep me from sinking into a roiling sea of fear as I watched them wheel him into the trauma center and straight down the hall toward an operating room.

"Are you a relative?" A woman with a clipboard found me staring at the closed doors. She was smiling and sympathetic, with round cheeks and short gray hair that stuck out as if she had forgotten to brush it that day.

"No. A friend."

"Why don't you sit down in the waiting room? We can talk there."

She ushered me to a brightly lit alcove with two couches upholstered in a blue floral fabric and a muted television tuned to "Jeopardy." I wasn't sure I should sit. I didn't want to get bloodstains on the sofa.

"Let me get you some clean towels," she said.

I didn't think I'd said anything, but maybe she was used to people in bloody clothes.

She settled me amid towels and brought out the clipboard

again. She stayed polite and sympathetic even when she discovered not only that I wasn't a relative, but that Curtis didn't have any relatives in Reno, and that I didn't know how to get in touch with his mother. I knew she was arriving in six days, but that was all. Some university official would have to provide the rest. And the information on his medical insurance.

"Help yourself to coffee and let me know if I can bring you anything else," she said. "Someone will tell you when he's out of surgery."

There was a large coffee urn on a table next to the television, with white foam cups and small packets of stuff surrounding it.

I closed my eyes to blot out Alex Trebek. I considered kicking out the screen, but I didn't have the energy.

"So what happened, O'Neal?"

The voice startled me. Somehow, as I had been sitting, my head had fallen over almost to my knees.

As much as I could be glad about anything, I was glad to see Matthews, the only homicide detective I felt more or less comfortable with.

"The kid shot Curtis, I shot the kid. That's all I know."

Matthews eased his bulk onto the other couch. He took off his heavy winter cap and slapped it against his knee.

"Was it robbery?"

"I think so. Curtis had just bought some earrings for his mother. The kid must have followed us from the jewelry store."

"Why'n't you just give him what he wanted? Why'd he shoot?"

"Oh, hell. I don't know. I guess Curtis didn't move fast enough, and the cowboys were coming, and the kid was scared."

" 'The kid'? You're thinking of the deceased malefactor as a kid?"

"That's all he was."

"Age, maybe. He was seventeen. But he was a mean, nasty, rotten human being. I checked him out." A meaty hand grasped my shoulder, forcing me upright. He fixed my eyes with his own large, watery blue ones. "Habitual truant. Two arrests for shoplifting. They let him go the first time when his mother paid for it, called it a misdemeanor the second time and put him on probation. A year ago he stuck a gun in the face of a convenience store clerk right under a video camera. He was released last week. I figure this is not only going to be ruled a justifiable homicide, we'll owe you a medal for saving the state a lot of time and money. The people who would have been victims of his future crimes owe you even more."

"Yeah. Sure. I guess you're right. Maybe I've even scared his brother straight."

"What brother?"

"Maybe it wasn't his brother. But somebody younger and shorter with the same general appearance was with him. Including the bad nerves. He ran before the shooting started."

"Anything else you didn't tell me?"

"Just that I saw them watching us, right before we left. I should have been more alert."

"And what? You would have drawn first?"

I shrugged. I didn't know how to answer that.

"I'll check on a brother," Matthews said. "Think you could pick him out of a lineup?"

"I can't promise, but I'll try." I had a brief fantasy of showing up with my nine millimeter Beretta and saving the state more money. I shook it away.

"How's Curtis doing?" he asked.

"They haven't told me."

He nodded, jowls sinking into the collar of his fleece-lined jacket and coming back up.

"Let me see what I can find out. And stop thinking of the shooter as a kid. You'll feel better."

I watched him lumber down the hall. I didn't want him to go.

My head was back on my knees when I heard somebody sit down. I jerked up, but it wasn't Matthews.

This man had to have been in the trauma center awhile, because he wasn't dressed for cold. His crewneck sweater with the red and green Christmas pattern cried out for an overcoat, and his smooth skin wasn't flushed. Lines appeared suddenly when he smiled, running from his cheeks to his square jaw, and his dark hair was graying. I placed him right around forty.

"Waiting's tough. Can I get you something?"

"I don't think so. Thanks." I dropped my head again, hoping he'd go away.

"I understand you have a friend in surgery."

"That's right. And I shot the guy who shot him. So you'll forgive me if I don't feel very sociable." A flash of hope arced through my brain and disappeared. I hadn't said kid. But I had still thought it.

"It's a painful situation. I wish I had some answers for you."

"I haven't asked you for any."

"I know. But I'm a minister, and I always wish I could offer them, even when I can't."

If I'd been feeling better, I might have tried to help him out. I shook my head and shut my eyes, hoping he'd go away.

He didn't leave, but he didn't say anything more.

"The odds are that your friend's gonna make it, O'Neal. It's serious—the bullet is close to his heart—but he's in good shape other than the bullet wound, and the intern was optimistic."

"Intern?" I jerked upright once more, hearing Matthews's voice.

"Yeah, she was all I could get. The surgeon's gonna be busy for another hour or so. She said his left lung collapsed, and whatever happens, he'll be in here for a while. And you could do worse than talk to Danken."

"What? Who's Danken?"

"The Reverend Michael Danken. The man sitting quietly across from you. Somebody's gotta walk you through the feelings, and he's got a lot of patience with that." He nodded solemnly at Danken, who nodded back, smiling.

"Will they let me see Curtis after the surgery?"

"I don't think so. So you might as well go home. He won't be awake anyway, and not likely to be before morning." Matthews put his hat on and tugged the earflaps down. "I don't think the DA will have a problem with self-defense, no charges filed. Stop by the station tomorrow afternoon and I'll let you know where we are with the brother."

"Yeah, sure." I watched him walk away again.

Danken was still silent.

"Did Matthews send you?" I asked.

"I was already here. Roy saw me talking to the admitting clerk and suggested I look for you."

That was the first time I had heard anybody refer to Matthews as Roy. Nobody ever used his first name.

"I appreciate your concern. And his, too. But I'm gonna wait until Curtis is out of surgery, and then I'm gonna go home." I hoped I could make it. I knew if I stayed for too long, I was going to pass out on the couch. I didn't want to give anybody an excuse to take my clothes and slap me into a hospital bed.

"Do you need a ride?"

I had forgotten that I didn't have a car.

"I can call a taxi. But thanks for asking."

I shut my eyes again.

I opened them to see a worried intern in bloody scrubs bending over to look at me.

"I'm okay," I said. "How's Curtis?"

"He did just fine in surgery. We'll be moving him to the intensive care ward in the main building tomorrow morning. Are you sure you're all right?"

"Yes. Thank you."

When she backed away, I saw that Danken was still sitting on the other couch. He smiled at me.

"Okay," I said. "I do need a ride. Thank you for waiting."

"Let's go, then."

We walked down the hall to the admitting area. Danken picked up an overcoat from a chair against the front counter, chatted briefly with the clipboard woman as he put it on, and led me back down the hall and around another corner before we went out through a side door.

The warmth of the trauma center had allowed me to build up a hazy insulation from everything that had happened. The drop in temperature shocked me out of it.

"Oh, hell," I whispered.

"This way," Danken said. "I think we'll be free of reporters. Kelly—the admitting clerk—warned me they were waiting just outside the front entrance."

We passed the front of the building as we crossed the narrow parking lot. Three television vans were parked in the street. Three camera crews were poised by the front door.

Danken opened the passenger door of still another mini-van and helped me in.

I let him.

"It'll be warm in a minute," he said when the motor was running and his seat belt was fastened. "Where to?"

I had to control my chattering teeth to give him directions. It wasn't far. If I hadn't been so cold, I could have walked.

My house was dark. I had expected to stay the night with Curtis, and I hadn't left a light on.

"Are you sure you'll be all right?" Danken asked.

"I'll do my best." I was still shivering, despite the heat in the van.

"I hope you'll call me if you change your mind and decide you'd like to talk about what happened." He pulled a card out of his pocket and handed it to me. "I've made myself available to several sworn peace officers who've been in similar situations. I'd like to be of help."

I took his card and handed him mine.

"I'll think about it. Thanks for the ride."

The van stayed at the curb until I had entered the house and turned on the lights.

The front room of my house is also my office. The message light was blinking on my answering machine, but whatever it was could wait. I stumbled down the hall to the bedroom.

Butch and Sundance had been sleeping so soundly that the light woke them up. They both blinked, surprised to see me. The fact that they were curled up more or less together was a comment about how much I had been gone lately.

Butch, a large, fluffy, gray tomcat, stretched and yawned, then moved slowly in my direction, away from his orange buddy. Petting him seemed like a good idea to both of us.

The phone rang and I grabbed it, sitting down sharply on the bed and startling both cats once again.

"Freddie? It's Mark Martin, Channel 12 News. Hey, I heard about what happened at the mall, and I'm really sorry. Is Curtis all right?"

"I think so. They wouldn't let me see him."

"God, I hope he's okay. He's such a great guy. We were all stunned to hear he'd been shot. According to the police, you saved his life. Listen, have you got a statement for us?"

"Oh, shit. No."

"I know you're upset. God, I would be if I'd shot somebody. But that was amazing, what you did, you know? Gunning down the bastard who shot your man? You gotta talk to us about it. Curtis would want you to. Horton will call you himself, if you want."

Curtis had done some consulting work with the station, and Horton Robb, the station owner and general manager, was his regular tennis partner. I wished that I knew what Curtis would want.

"I'll think about it. I'll call you tomorrow. Or Lane. I'll call Lane tomorrow."

"Lane? An exclusive interview? He'd love it! Great! Get a good night's sleep, and we'll see you at the station tomorrow."

Mark had turned that into more than I intended. I had grasped at the idea of Lane Josten, the Channel 12 news anchor, because I thought he might help me figure out a way to deal with what would clearly be media interest in the situation. He and Sandra Herrick, my friend who worked for the *Nevada Herald*. If I did an exclusive interview, it would go to her.

An exclusive interview. Shit. I was so tired I was listening to Mark Martin and taking him seriously. I didn't have anything to say to anybody, not my few friends, still less an indifferent, if curious, public.

The phone rang again. This time I ignored it.

This wasn't a goddamn media event. This was my own personal crisis. And I couldn't think of a person I wanted to share it with. Except the one who was in the trauma center.

I unplugged the bedroom phone and turned off the light.

In the dark, I took off my clothes and crawled under the covers.

Butch started kneading my shoulder, and Sundance re-settled himself against my knees.

I'm not a religious person, and I don't know how to pray. So I begged whatever powers exist in the universe that I could go to sleep and wake up in the morning to find everything the way it had been the morning before.

I guess nothing heard me.

In the morning, Curtis was still in the hospital and the kid was still dead.

Chapter
3

AN INSISTENT DOORBELL finally forced me out of bed.

I scattered the cats, grabbed my bathrobe, and staggered down the hall.

Fortunately I checked the peephole before flinging open the door. I didn't recognize the guy, but the microphone in his hand and the cameraman behind him gave away his identity.

The phone on the desk was ringing. I didn't care. I staggered back to bed, where I couldn't hear it.

The reporter rang the doorbell three more times before he gave up.

I plugged the bedroom phone back in, cut off the reporter who was leaving a message, and called Deke.

"Listen, I hope I didn't wake you."

Deke worked the graveyard shift at the Mother Lode casino as a security guard. The digital clock said 10:05, and he usually went to bed about ten.

"Wake me up? Don't you check your messages? I been waiting for hours to hear from you!"

"I'm sorry. I unplugged the bedroom phone, and I haven't

checked messages. I think I need a bodyguard. Are you available?"

"In about fifteen minutes. I'll ring the front bell two long and three short."

"Bring coffee."

"I would have anyway. I'm not drinking that instant swill you serve. How's Curtis?"

"He was still alive last night."

I hung up and called the hospital. Curtis had done well in surgery, as the intern had told me, and was currently in intensive care, condition serious but vital signs stable. And hospital policy was serious, too. I couldn't see him because I wasn't a relative.

I wanted to slam the phone in the nurse's ear. But I happened to look at my hand. The paramedic hadn't done a complete job of cleaning the blood off. I had to take a shower.

When I was clean and dry, I checked the sweater, jeans, and jacket still lying on the floor where I had dropped them. Bloodstained, all of them.

I found clean jeans and a clean sweater in my dresser. And I was suddenly grateful for small favors.

I was barely dressed by the time Deke arrived.

"Curtis is alive, but they won't let me see him," I said as Deke handed me a cardboard cup. I set it down on my desk and pulled the top off, almost scalding myself on the steam. My stomach gurgled, reminding me that there was nothing to absorb the coffee but acid. I hadn't gotten around to eating the night before. Eating or anything else. The light on the answering machine was still blinking. "And I guess I need to check my messages."

"I'll sit," he said, dropping heavily into one of the black-and-white cowhide client chairs.

All messages were from reporters, except those from Deke, Sandra, and my mother. And Sandra was a reporter as well as a friend.

"I have to call Ramona," I said, trying to gather the courage.

"I'll call and tell her Curtis is alive and you're sedated."

"Would you?"

He reached across the desk for the phone, but I stopped him.

"That's a lie. Just tell her Curtis is alive and I'm okay and I'll call when I can."

"That isn't a lie?"

"It's as close to the truth as I can give her right now."

I slunk off to the kitchen, feeling some guilt. But not enough to call her myself. I would have had to reassure her that I was all right, and I wasn't confident enough to do that. Deke would do a better job. And he could keep her from coming down here.

Ramona and Al lived at Lake Tahoe, about an hour's drive away when the roads weren't too icy to drive. Al had stayed pretty close to home since his heart attack three months ago, and I was certain Ramona would be happy to be talked into staying with him.

The refrigerator held moldy Chinese take-out, dried-out pizza, a few condiments, and three cans of beer.

Furry bodies rubbing against my legs reminded me that there was cat food in the cupboard.

I split a can of a noxious-smelling substance labeled Turkey Parts between two bowls, refilled two more bowls from a twenty-pound sack of crunchies, and topped off their water bowl. Whether I ate or not, my cats were well cared for. And they purred as they buried their noses in their breakfasts, to let me know they appreciated that.

"Sandra's meeting us at the Mother Lode." Deke appeared in the doorway. "She's been pretty worried about not hearing from you, and I didn't think you'd want to put her off."

I thought about getting mad that he'd called Sandra without asking. But I couldn't afford to have Deke mad at me, not just then. Anyway, he was right. It wasn't fair to put Sandra off.

"What about Ramona?"

"She isn't happy, but she'll wait for you to call."

"Okay. Thanks. And it's probably good that you called Sandra. I need something to eat, and there isn't anything here. Besides that, I'll only have to tell the two of you once. I'm not sure how many times I want to tell the story."

"You want to tell it a lot. You want to tell it as many times as you have to tell it until it doesn't hurt you anymore."

I wanted to tell him I was fine, that it already didn't hurt too much, but a strange sound came out of my throat.

I held onto the sink until I could talk.

"Can you get me past the reporters?"

"I already told them, anybody who rushes you when we leave the house gets slapped with a harassment suit. That won't stop them from shouting, but it may keep them across the street."

"Okay. Let's go."

Deke waited by the front door while I decided whether I needed a coat. The morning wasn't really that cold, and the faded denim jacket I'd been wearing the day before was too bloody to look at. I figured I'd be either indoors or in the sun. The sweater was wool. No coat.

I put the lid back on my coffee, to take it with me.

Outside, I was assaulted by the noise. But Deke was right—they held up their cameras and kept their distance.

He had parked his black Ford pickup behind my Jeep. He backed it out of the driveway so sharply that he might have wanted to graze somebody.

I almost asked him to drive carefully.

He took us down Mill to Center Street, then the few blocks across the Truckee to the Mother Lode, and around the corner into the parking structure. It was usually an easy walk—easier to walk than to drive, with all the construction going on all the time. I did it three or four nights a week to meet Deke for dinner. I couldn't have made it that day.

We walked across the alley and passed through the air curtain into the casino. Because casinos never close, they don't need doors, and some don't have them. Air curtains are surprisingly good insulation, even in winter. The temperature inside had to be thirty degrees warmer. I was glad I had skipped the coat.

I let Deke open a path through the sullen tourists, the midmorning slot players trying to recoup from the night before. The hair of the gambling dog.

Some might have been there for days. Without clocks, they might have slipped into the eternal now of casino time, hearts beating to the red neon flashing jackpot lights, ears ringing with the buzzer for the change girl, noses stinging in the stale, smoky air. The lure was suddenly clear to me. I had grown old overnight, and I wanted as never before to stop time.

If Deke had looked back before stepping onto the escalator to the coffee shop, I might have stayed in Hades. But he trusted, and I followed.

Sandra was waiting in a corner booth. She waved, tentatively. I couldn't remember seeing Sandra tentative before.

"How are you? How's Curtis?" she asked when I sat

down next to her, sliding around the curve of the red vinyl seat.

"He's alive. And I am, too." It was lame, but I couldn't come up with anything sharp.

She pushed a copy of the *Herald* toward me. "In case you haven't seen it."

A story below the fold on the front page was headlined UNIVERSITY PROFESSOR SHOT AT MALL. The subhead was PI GIRLFRIEND KILLS GUNMAN.

The police beat reporter had talked to one of the cowboys, the mall security guard, a spokesman for the hospital, Curtis's department chair, and Matthews. The only new information was that Alan Laird, the chair, was stunned. And that Matthews had a higher opinion of me than I had been aware of.

"We'd like a quote from you, obviously," Sandra said. "But anything you want to say off the record stays there, you know that."

Deke landed with a thud on the other side of me. The three of us suddenly took up space for four.

"I told the cashier to call security if she sees a camera," he said.

I nodded, waited for the waitress to fill our coffee cups, and turned back to Sandra. "Two kids, one with a gun, stopped us in the parking lot. Curtis got shot. I killed the kid. The reporter got it right, except he didn't mention the other kid."

"Don't call him a kid," Deke said, in the same tone Matthews had used the night before. "A teenager with a pointed gun isn't a kid anymore."

"I saw him, Deke. He sure looked like one scared, desperate kid to me. And there isn't a kid anymore."

"I checked with both the *Herald* receptionist and the one

at Channel 12. Every caller has been supportive. Almost."
She took a sip of her coffee, and I waited. "Well, his mother
called, of course."

"What's her name?" When Sandra didn't answer, I added,
"She'll be on tonight's news."

I realized then that I wanted to know the kid's name. I knew
Deke wouldn't like it, and Matthews—Roy—wouldn't like it,
but I had to know the kid's name.

"Elva Morales. Her son's name was Jamie. You don't
really want to know anything about them, do you?"

"I guess not. I'm not sure, though. Maybe I do."

Sandra patted my hand. "Is there anything you want to
say for some kind of public statement?"

"Just that I didn't mean to kill him."

I know my face twisted when I said it, because Sandra
and Deke each grabbed one shoulder.

"You had to," they said at almost the same time. But the
words were off-key and out of sync. I couldn't process
them.

"Ready to order, or do you need a little more time?" the
cheery waitress asked. When we all turned to stare, she
flinched.

Sandra and Deke had both eaten earlier. They looked at
me.

"Toast," I said. "I could handle toast."

"Bring scrambled eggs, sausage, and home fries," Deke
said. "Just in case."

"How long are the cameras going to follow me?" I asked
Sandra.

"It depends. If you're lucky, a psycho will blow up the
championship bowling alley this afternoon, leaving nine
dead, unable to pick up the spare, and the hounds will have
a new scent to follow."

"That's gross," I said.

"You almost smiled."

"It was still gross."

"What she's saying is, hang in," Deke said. "You'll be yesterday's hero real soon."

"As long as that's what you want," Sandra added.

"What do you mean?"

"Well, one of the sagebrush militias will probably try to recruit you for a poster child. If Jamie Morales had thought you might be armed, would he have drawn his gun? If not, then more citizens need guns."

"No," I said. "I don't want to be anybody's poster child. And I certainly don't want to argue for the right of every citizen to carry a concealed weapon. The attempt to bring law and order to the West meant taking guns away from teenaged sociopaths. I don't know what happened in the last hundred years so that we're giving them back."

"Militias aren't arguing for armed kids," Deke said.

"Whatever. I don't know what to do next, but I don't think the private military groups are the answer."

I thought briefly of my father and the gunrunners he had worked for. The only thought that could possibly have made my day worse.

"Be careful about calling Jamie Morales a teenaged sociopath in public. His mother might take serious offense, and while that might not hurt your case, it surely won't help it," Sandra said.

"Oh, God. Deep shit getting deeper."

"And it will, unless you figure out what to say to your public," Deke said. "A lot of good people in this state are going to be pointing out that if you hadn't had a gun, and known how to use it, you and Curtis might both be dead. And they'll be pretty close to right. Would you rather it was you or Billy the Kid in the morgue?"

"Him, I guess. Ask me again next week, okay? And you said not to think of him as a kid."

"Thinking about Billy the Kid might help. Now there was a teenaged sociopath. That's what used to be called a juvenile delinquent, right?"

"Yeah. But his mother probably wouldn't like that, either."

"Why were you carrying your gun?" Sandra asked. "You don't always have it in your boot."

"I had to repo a car yesterday afternoon. I never got around to putting the gun away. If I'd thought about it, I wouldn't have been armed."

There was a long silence after that, while I nibbled a piece of toast and they both stared at their coffee. Deke finally started in on the eggs. Watching him eat, I decided I could handle a sausage link and some of the fries.

"Is there anything I can do?" Sandra finally asked.

"Do you think I should offer to give some kind of statement to Lane?"

"Well, if you did, the rest would probably go away fairly quickly, having been scooped. And at least you'd be dealing with a friendly face."

"Okay. Then you could call him and set it up."

"I'll be right back," she said, sliding out of the booth.

"How about some more toast?" Deke asked.

"I've had enough, thanks. If I have to deal with a television camera, I don't want too much in my stomach."

"If you don't want to do it, you could hide out at my place for a while, till all this goes away."

"Thanks again. But if Sandra's right, and talking to Lane gets rid of the others, then that's what I want to do. If you want to go home, though—I know it's past your bedtime—I can manage."

He screwed his face into a menacing frown. "I said I'd be

your bodyguard. That means when you see Matthews, when you see Sandra's blow-dried buddy, when you see whoever else you need to see. Bodyguard means I'm with you until you're safe inside your house, and I sleep on the couch if I think there might be trouble."

"I don't know how many times I can say thanks."

"Once covers the whole day."

I nibbled some more toast. "Did you know the gunfight at the O.K. Corral was about whether private citizens could carry weapons?"

"I think I saw that in a movie."

Sandra was on her way back, waving a slip of paper.

"Three o'clock this afternoon, at the studio. You'll both have time for a nap first."

"Are you sure you don't mind coming with me?" I asked Deke. "I said I'd see Matthews this afternoon. You could take a nap on my bed for a couple of hours, and then we could go from the police station to the television studio."

"Sounds good," Deke said.

"I'll be at my desk if you want to run anything past me—something like a prepared statement that doesn't slander the deceased." Sandra had been sitting still long enough, and I knew she was restless to get back to work.

"Can't slander scum," Deke said.

"No, but Sandra's right. I want to calm things down, not fire them up. I have to think about what I'm going to say. Except that I'm sorry he's dead."

Sandra grabbed the check and stood. "On the *Herald.* Talk to you later. Call as soon as you hear anything about Curtis."

"Oh, God," I groaned again. "I still haven't called my mother, and I have to find out how to call his. That's the only way I'll ever get in to see him, and I need to see him."

I almost bit my tongue trying to take the words back. But I did need to see him.

"You make phone calls, I nap," Deke said. "Let's go."

I followed them out with the sinking feeling that whatever I did next was going to make things worse.

Chapter
4

THE JUNGLE DRUMS must have been beating after Sandra called Lane, because the news vans were gone from in front of my house.

I let Deke find his own way to the bedroom while I stared at the blinking red light on my answering machine.

Two tabloid reporters wanted to pay for my story, seven decent citizens wanted to offer congratulations on my marksmanship, one cryptic voice identifying himself as Baxter Cate wanted my participation in a deal of possible mutual benefit, two potential clients wanted bodyguards, and the Reverend Michael Danken wanted to make sure I was all right.

I wrote down the numbers of the two potential clients. I already had Danken's number, the decent citizens didn't expect return calls, and the other three could forget it.

But the next thing I did was call Richmond, Virginia, information to see if Curtis's mother had a listed number, something I would have done the night before if I'd been in my right mind. There was a listing for a T. R. Breckinridge, and I decided that was close enough to Tola Rae. I tried the number.

When a voice with a soft drawl informed me that Mrs. Breckinridge was unavailable, I explained who I was and where I was calling from.

"Well, then, you can probably see her a few hours from now," the voice said. "She's already left for the airport here, and she'll be landing at the Reno airport at ten-fifteen this evening, your time. Can you tell me how Curtis is?"

"The last I heard he was in serious condition, but they expect him to live. They won't let me see him. I thought she wasn't coming until next week."

"She changed her plans when the hospital called."

"Do you have her flight number?"

"No, but I know she has to change in St. Louis. When you see Curtis, would you tell him Patelaine sends her love?"

"Sure. And thanks for the information." I hoped that it was just my trustworthy voice, and that the woman with the drawl wouldn't tell five reporters when Curtis's mother was arriving. I was too tired to wonder who Patelaine was.

I was too tired to call Ramona, too, but I bit the bullet and did it anyway.

"Freddie! My God! I have been so worried! The morning paper said just enough to terrify me! When I couldn't reach you by phone, Al said he'd be all right if I left for a few hours, and I was just getting ready to drive down to look for you when Deke called."

"I'm okay, Ramona. You don't have to be worried."

"The paper said you killed the boy who shot Curtis—they didn't identify him because he was a minor—and you have to be upset about that. I called the hospital, and they told me Curtis was probably going to live. I'm certain he will. At least one thing will come out right."

"Yes, sure. And you're right. I'm upset. I didn't intend to

kill the boy." I made an effort to calm my heart, to keep my blood pressure from spiking.

"I knew that. And I knew it was going to happen sooner or later. You're in a profession where people are always getting killed. It was only a matter of time before you had to shoot in self-defense. I'm only glad you were prepared to do it, and I hope you aren't blaming yourself for that dead teenager's problems. His mother was on television this morning, such a pathetic woman. I felt so sorry for her. Do you want me to come down there? Deke said to wait until I talked to you, but I could drive down if you need me."

The spirit of Christmas was clicking in early.

"No, don't do that. Really. I'm grateful that you would, but please don't do that. Al needs you, and I'm doing all right. Deke's here, and I have stuff to take care of this afternoon."

"I'm glad Deke's there. Will you give my love to Curtis?"

"As soon as I see him. And I'll call you afterwards."

"You know, if you were married to him, you could visit him in intensive care. You wouldn't have to go through this terrible waiting, you know that. And then he might help you get a job at the university, one where you wouldn't have to carry a gun."

I fought the urge to yell at her. She was in her cozy little chalet, fire going in the fireplace, and the only way she could deal with a serious situation was to talk it to death.

"I've only known him six months. I think this is a little premature."

"Well, think about it later. How much easier it would be if you were married. You could take your time looking for a different job."

"I'll think about it. Later. Now I have to go. I have to make a formal statement to the police."

That was the wrong thing to say.

"They aren't charging you with anything, are they? This was clearly self-defense, or Curtis's defense, or something like that. I'll have Al call someone in the district attorney's office. And he knows several lawyers with connections, if David is stubborn for some reason. I can't imagine that he would be—he wants to run for governor, you know."

"I think it'll be okay, Ramona. I'll call you. Don't ask Al to call anybody. Promise?"

It took a little longer, but I pushed her into hanging up peacefully.

David Guerin, the Washoe County district attorney, certainly talked to the newspapers as if he were planning to run for governor. And Al Butler, Ramona's husband, was Lake Tahoe's state assemblyman. It was a connection of sorts, but one I didn't want to pursue. Besides, my gut was telling me I'd be better off letting Matthews make my case. If I could make things worse, Ramona could turn a tough situation into a cataclysm.

And maybe a case didn't need to be made.

I hadn't intended to kill anybody. If Curtis hadn't been shot, if I hadn't been afraid for both our lives, I wouldn't have gone for my gun. Surely Guerin would understand that.

If I hadn't been lazy, I wouldn't even have had the gun with me.

I picked up the phone again.

The Reverend Michael Danken answered.

"I'm doing okay," I told him. "I just wanted to thank you for being concerned."

"I'm glad you called, Freddie." His voice was so steady that I felt easier just hearing it. "I've seen police officers react to traumatic stress the way you did last night—a calm exterior covering inner turmoil. The ones who come out of it most easily are the ones who have human support. I wanted to make certain you felt supported and that you weren't alone."

"Thank you. That was really kind of you." I had to stop because my throat clutched.

"Would you mind if I made a suggestion?"

"Not at all." I got it out on a short breath.

"If you think doing a few good deeds for others might help atone for the life lost last night—not because you did anything bad, or wrong, but simply to acknowledge the value of that life—I could start you off by introducing you to a woman who needs your services but lacks the ability to pay for them."

"If you're telling me that there's always somebody whose problems are worse, I know that."

"Her problems aren't worse. In fact, they're more easily solved. I thought you might like that."

"You're right. I do. But I can't deal with her today."

"You don't have to make an appointment now. I just wanted you to know that you can make a positive difference to someone."

"You're persuasive, Reverend. I'll call again when I can."

I had almost agreed to dash right over. But I was feeling too vulnerable. And I would have had to wake up Deke.

I called the hospital again, just to hear that Curtis was still alive. The woman sounded tired. She said his condition was unchanged, and I didn't pursue it.

Butch had climbed onto my lap at some point. I dug my fingers into his thick, gray fur and massaged his spine. At least he didn't want anything I couldn't give.

I slid a notepad that my local councilman had given out last time he was running for office to the center of my desk and picked up a pen. Sandra was right. I needed to think through—even write down—what I wanted to say before I got in front of a camera. I didn't want to turn on the computer and open a file, because then I'd feel compelled to check my e-mail, see if any work had piled up. I knew that any PIs in my network who had heard about the shooting would be supportive, and that was enough. Besides, it felt right to do this by hand.

But no words came. I had shot to defend Curtis, to defend myself. I could just say that, and remember not to call the kid—Jamie Morales—a sociopath. After all, I didn't know him. I could even express remorse. And Lane wouldn't ask tough questions anyway. He didn't know how. I could get through this, and the reporters would be gone.

My head was down on the desk when Deke touched my shoulder.

"If you want to see Matthews before we go to the television station, we got to leave now."

"Okay."

"And don't look for your bloody clothes. I took them."

"Okay. Thanks."

I pushed Butch off my lap and followed Deke to the truck. I knew there had been a time when I had energy, when I could lead as well as follow. I wondered how long it would take me to get it back.

Deke drove the two blocks to the police station and dropped me off in front.

I nodded at Danny Sinclair, the red-haired desk sergeant. He had the courtesy to nod back, even though we had never liked each other.

I walked past a scraggly Christmas tree, headed down the hall to the detectives' room, and found Matthews at his desk. He pulled my All American out of a drawer and slid it toward me. He handed me the unused bullets in an envelope.

"No charges," he said. "You shot in self-defense and you had a license for a gun. It's official. Take a look at this."

He handed me a yellow card with six mug shots pasted onto it, all dark-haired teenaged boys.

"Bottom row middle," I told him.

"You sure?"

"Yeah."

"We'll do a lineup with his attorney present. Tomorrow morning at ten."

"It's the brother, isn't it?"

"See you then, O'Neal."

I slipped my gun back into my boot and left.

I didn't look at Danny Sinclair on my way out.

Deke was standing on the front steps, waiting. I made an effort to walk ahead of him to the truck.

"Do we have time to make a stop?" I asked. I was still thinking about the Reverend Danken, and the easy problem.

"No. Can it wait?"

"Yeah. Later."

We rode across town to the television studio in silence. I didn't tell him about the brother.

Deke wanted to drop me at the door again, but I insisted on having him come in with me. The parking lot wasn't crowded, and he pulled in next to the program director's red Corvette.

I got out and waited while he locked the pickup. The winter had so far been unusually mild and snowless. There was a faint white dust on the Sierras, but the sky was a bright, sharp blue, and the sun was radiating the strange high-altitude heat that burns people on the ski slopes, the kind that can fool you into thinking the air isn't really cold. A fat moon looked like a windblown ball of white dandelion fluff hanging close to the horizon.

The day was so beautiful it made my heart ache worse.

Deke was waiting for me when I turned around. He

followed me from the asphalt to the gravel walk to the glass doors.

"Sweetheart! Are you okay?" Lane Josten was standing just inside. He hugged me before I could protest.

Not that I would have protested too much. Lane was a black-haired, blue-eyed hunk with a skier's tan and an irresistible smile, and he gave great hugs.

The receptionist glared at me stiffly over Lane's shoulder. Somebody needed to tell her that she wasn't Lane's type, but it wouldn't be me. I kissed him on the cheek.

"I'm hanging in," I told him.

"How's Curtis?"

"Still alive."

"Come with me. We'll talk while you're in makeup."

He laced his fingers through mine and dragged me past the sour-faced receptionist and the bushy, tinseled tree.

"Deke—"

"I'll wait here," he said, settling himself onto a couch. "I don't need makeup."

"Lane, I don't want makeup. I want to look sick and pale for this one."

"Are you sure?" He looked at me as if he couldn't imagine wanting to look sick and pale for anything.

"I'm sure. And we don't need to talk before we go before the camera. I'll tell you what happened, express remorse, and that's it."

"All right. Studio C it is."

It was half a corridor away. Two cameras were waiting, men attached. The lights were already focused on two amorphous black chairs with a table between them. Lane sat in one, I took the other, threading the microphone under my sweater. I knew the drill.

"You're going to look pale," the floor manager warned. "And that brown sweater isn't going to show up very well."

"No problem," I said. I hoped I wouldn't start to sweat. I wanted to look contrite, not guilty.

The first couple of questions went as planned. I told Lane what had happened—how Curtis fell, how threatened I felt—and said I was sorry.

"What would you do differently if you could do it over?" he asked.

I should have been prepared for that, of course. It was exactly the kind of slow ball down the middle that Lane would pitch to me. But I was tired and stressed and I broke the bat.

"What would *I* do differently? *I* didn't do anything wrong." The words sounded hard, even to me. "What should I have done—shopped at a different mall? Knowing what I know now, what I'd do differently is shoot first. Both of them, if I had to, to save Curtis."

"That sounds as if you think Curtis Breckinridge's life is worth two others. Do you really want to say that?" Lane's handsome brow was furrowed.

"Hell, yes, I think he's worth two of them. Two of anybody. A wonderful person is in the hospital, in pain, and still in some danger for his life, because nobody—no parent—taught two teenaged boys that stealing is wrong. Wrong. Absolutely wrong. This is not some culturally relative value judgment, this is an ethical absolute. Robbing people at gunpoint is wrong. We cannot live together, cannot call this a civilized society, unless we all agree to that. Am I sorry Jamie Morales is dead? Of course. Would I shoot him again to save Curtis? You bet. Ten times over."

I knew from the concern on Lane's face that I had gone too far. I had thought I was going to defuse the situation, but I had just screwed up, and he wasn't going to be able to convince anybody to edit it out.

"I think that's all I have to ask you," he said.

How seriously I had screwed up became clear when Horton Robb burst into the studio, rubbing his hands and chuckling. He looked like a gargoyle with a gray brush cut. If gargoyles wore Italian wool suits.

"By God, Freddie, that was terrific. An anthem. If the dead bastard's mother files a lawsuit, I'll start a fund for your defense."

"Thanks, Horton," I whispered. I was losing my voice five minutes too late.

I unhooked the microphone and stood up.

Lane followed me out to the hall.

"What can I do?" he asked.

"Contribute to my defense fund, I guess. You didn't do anything."

"If it helps, I think you're right."

"I think I'm right, too. But if Horton's happy, I've somehow gone too far right—I went beyond advocating law and order to advocating vigilantism. I didn't intend to do that, and I don't like the company I'm keeping."

"Don't start lobbing dud bombs at the IRS," he said.

He knew it was a feeble joke—a reference to one of last year's big stories, when two militia members couldn't even build an effective bomb to blow up an Internal Revenue Service office. I smiled anyway.

"With my luck, I'd only blow myself up."

Lane picked up my hand and walked me back to the lobby. I'm not big on physical contact, but Lane somehow made it okay.

Deke had been sitting with his eyes closed. I had to get him home soon, or he wouldn't make it through his shift.

"How'd you do?" he asked.

"I started fine, but I forgot I was here to make nice. Now we have to make the other stop."

I said good-bye to Lane and we trudged back to the

pickup. Deke didn't ask where we were going until the motor was running.

"First Church of the Inner Christ," I said.

"Pray if you got to," he answered. "Can't hurt."

"I don't know about that, but I've got to talk to the minister."

"Danken? I heard about him."

"You did? What?"

"I heard he talked down a suicidal cop last year, one ready to eat his gun. Your friend Matthews probably could tell you the story."

"Yeah, probably."

The small squat building with big antennas that housed Channel 12's studio was on Oddie Boulevard. Deke drove the pickup to 395 South and took the Second Street exit in silence. He dropped down Wells to Ryland and slowed in front of the church. Actually, it was a small brick house with a sign calling it a church. And it was only a couple of blocks from Washoe Medical. Not a bad location for a minister with a calling to visit the sick and wounded.

"I can walk home," I said. "And you have to get some sleep."

"You sure you won't need a bodyguard after the news?"

"Need one? I am one. And I have my gun."

He shook his head. "And more trouble if you use it."

"Matthews unloaded it, anyway."

"I'll just pull into that space ahead."

"All right, you can wait. This shouldn't take long. But then you drop me off at home." I didn't remind him that I had to meet Tola Rae Breckinridge at the airport. I needed to be alone for that.

"Deal."

I wasn't certain how to approach what was clearly a

combination church and home. A sign on the door helped me out.

"Welcome, Friend. Our regular office hours are from ten to six, seven days a week. During those hours, you may enter without knocking. Outside those hours, please ring the bell. Church services are held Sunday mornings at eleven. Prayer meetings are Wednesday evenings at seven. All are welcome."

I was there during office hours. I opened the door without knocking and walked into a room with a small altar at one end, arranged around an old brick fireplace. One row of folding chairs was set up to face it. What appeared to be four or five more rows' worth leaned against the walls. It wasn't much of a church, but something there felt good. Something made it peaceful underneath the tacked-up Christmas cards and the looping garlands. Two small trees sat on either side of the altar in wide pots. The few silver bells hanging from the branches almost looked natural.

"May I help you?"

The speaker stood framed in an archway leading to the rest of the house. She was a fortyish woman who reminded me a bit of Annette Funicello during her peanut butter commercial days, after she stopped doing beach movies, but before she got sick. The dark hair in a round wave falling almost to her shoulder, the dark eyebrows, the bright, dimpled smile.

"I'm looking for the Reverend Danken."

"I'll get him. I'm Louise Danken, his wife."

When I told her who I was, I was afraid she was going to rush over and hug me. I stepped back. I had been hugged enough.

She just nodded, smiling, and retreated to the hall.

I heard her call, "Mike?"

He was in the archway almost immediately.

"I was just starting dinner. Can you stay?"

I thought about how little I had had to eat. I thought about Deke waiting.

"I'll take a rain check," I said. "I just wanted to know about the woman with the easily solved problem. Could you set up a meeting?"

"Of course. Tomorrow afternoon?"

"Fine. And I need you to set up another meeting, too." I paused, but he waited me out. "I want to talk to Elva Morales, the dead kid's mother."

"That shouldn't be hard," he said. "In fact, the woman I want you to meet is her cousin."

I was still alert enough that warning bells went off in my head when he told me that. But I wasn't alert enough to refuse.

"I hope this works" was all I said.

"I know you do. And so do I. More than that, I believe that sometimes—often—good arises out of evil, that what seems our darkest trial is in fact our most important lesson. I hope I can persuade you that I'm right." He smiled, and I wanted him to be right.

"Okay. I'll see you tomorrow."

I was shaking when I got back to the car.

"Just get me home," I said to Deke. "I need to take a nap."

Chapter
5

I RECOGNIZED TOLA Rae Breckinridge as she stepped out of the jetway. She was the one in the short mink coat that was probably fine for Virginia winters but was surely going to leave her feeling the chill in Reno. Especially since she was wearing a knee-length skirt and sheer nylons that left her thin legs exposed. And no hat covered her blond bob, cut straight at the chin line.

I met her just inside the gate and introduced myself.

She held out a bony hand to shake mine, without much energy.

"Thank you for coming," she said. "I've been looking forward to meeting you."

Because Curtis was so tall, I had expected her to be taller. But her head barely came to my shoulder, even though she was wearing three-inch heels. Otherwise, she looked like the photograph Curtis had showed me. Large, dark blue eyes, high cheekbones, slightly pointed chin, and amazing, translucent skin that might have been coated with a drop or two of very expensive makeup.

"Yes. Thank you. I'm sorry . . ." I struggled until she cut me off.

"Is the hospital far?"

"Not really."

"Then—if you don't mind—I'd like to get my bags and go right over."

She pushed her hair behind her right ear. She was wearing pearl studs, but the sapphire studs would have been perfect, too. They would have matched her eyes. A casual glance took in and dismissed the double row of welcome-to-Reno slot machines.

"This way," I said, redundantly, since there wasn't any other way to go.

We walked along the corridor toward the escalator, past the posters with painted neon hawking hotel-casinos, and the posters with posed university professors hawking the more intellectual attractions. Past the protect-your-assets, incorporate-in-Nevada poster. Past the 1931 LaSalle from the automotive museum. Past the souvenir shops and the Christmas decorations. In silence.

We waited in silence until the luggage from her flight began to hit the carousel. She pointed out two matching pieces of Louis Vuitton, and I grabbed them when they got around to us.

"You might want to wait inside while I get the Jeep," I said.

"Not unless it's a very large parking lot. I've been waiting too many hours now."

"It's actually a very small parking lot for something that bills itself as an international airport. But even a short walk is bad when you're not prepared for the cold."

"I'm prepared for the worst," she answered. "The chill won't bother me."

"Please don't say that, Mrs. Breckinridge. I really believe Curtis is going to be fine."

She patted my arm. "Tola Rae. Call me Tola Rae. I believe that, too, that Curtis will be fine. I prepare for the worst, but I hope for the best."

Tola Rae caught her breath sharply when the automatic glass door opened and the cold air hit her lungs. Then she stepped forward, her high heels drumming the sidewalk with a sharp, stoic beat. I threaded a path between waiting taxis to the short-term parking. The Jeep was parked in the second row of meters.

I helped her into the passenger side and tossed her bags in the back. She stifled a wince as something thudded.

"It'll warm up in a minute," I said once I had trotted around to the driver's side and started the motor. "Have you thought about where you might stay?"

"Curtis's place, of course. His keys should be at the hospital, with the rest of his belongings. I'm sure you can help me find the apartment."

"Yes. Of course."

I was turning onto Kietzke Lane before I gave up trying to figure out whether there was an edge in what she had said. She didn't have anything that I would call a Southern accent—eight years in New England for prep school and college would have taken care of that—but her voice was quiet, lilting, and I had the feeling that if she ever really had it in for me, I wouldn't discover I'd been hit till I was out cold.

"Could you tell me what happened? All the hospital said was that Curtis had been shot."

I took a deep breath and started at the mall, telling it the way I had told it before. She interrupted once, with an "Oh, dear, how awful," when she heard that Jamie Morales was dead, and I did fine until I got to the place where I was sitting on the trauma center couch and Curtis was in surgery.

My teeth began to chatter and I had to pull over. Tola Rae placed her left hand over my right one, on the steering wheel. I think she had meant to hold it, but I couldn't get my fingers loose enough to respond.

"Are you all right?" she asked.

"I thought I was. I will be in a minute."

"I must have seemed very inconsiderate, not to have said something earlier. I wish I had been warned. This has to be a terrible experience for you as well as for Curtis."

And I hadn't even gotten to the phone calls and the television appearance. The evening news had prompted more calls, but I had ignored them all, including Ramona's. Anyway, most were from good ol' boys who wanted to buy me a drink and share the vicarious thrill of the shoot.

"Yes. Thank you. It is."

"All I can tell you is, what doesn't kill us, makes us stronger."

Tola Rae left her hand on mine until I stopped shaking. I pulled away from the curb and drove on to the medical center.

I wanted to drop her at the entrance, but she insisted on staying with me until I found a space in the lot.

"Will my bags be safe here?" she asked.

"I can't promise, but I think so. There's a man in the information booth, nobody can see the bags without getting up close with a flashlight, and any burglars working this lot will probably be looking to hit a better car than a Jeep."

She nodded and got out. I had to admire her for appearing to be so frail and acting so determined.

The few yards to the main door felt like a long trek.

Once inside, Tola Rae handled things with an authority that had to have been born of long practice.

I suspect Washoe Medical is better than most hospitals.

The grand piano with the sign inviting you to play has to be one of a kind. And the warm colors, the alcoves, the urns of coffee are comforting, even overlaid with tinsel. Nevertheless, hospitals tend to take the life out of a person, in spirit if not in fact. The people in uniform behave as if they know how to run your life better than you do, and it's hard to argue, even if you're not sick.

But Tola Rae had the uniforms running around finding the intern from the night before, finding Curtis's things, finding the unfinished forms. Somebody offered her coffee and then actually brought it.

And all this was between the front desk and the intensive care waiting room right down the hall.

The intern still wouldn't let me out of the waiting room. And Tola Rae was only allowed fifteen minutes. Fear of infection. And Curtis was asleep anyway.

The door between the waiting room and the ward itself was solid. I tried to look for him when Tola Rae went in, but all I could see was a curtain.

I sat on a sofa upholstered in green with peach cabbage roses. A fat woman with patchy, dyed brown hair, so thin you could see her scalp, sat across from me.

Lane Josten smiled mutely from the television set. I thought about turning the sound up, but I couldn't think of anything I wanted to hear.

When Tola Rae came back out, her eyes were red.

"Let's go," she said. "I'll come back in the morning. And I've told them that you should be treated as family. If you come tomorrow, they'll let you in."

Tola Rae was almost to the front door before I could say I appreciated what she was doing.

I was too tired to chat with her on the way to Curtis's apartment, and she must have felt the same.

I stopped in the red zone in front of the entrance and pulled her luggage out of the back.

"You don't have to see me in," she said. "And tomorrow I'll use Curtis's car. Can you tell me where it is?"

"Oh, hell. It's probably still in the mall parking lot. I'll pick you up in the morning and drive you over."

"I don't want you to do that. I have the keys, and it shouldn't be hard to find if I go before the stores are open. I'll simply call a taxi when I'm ready to go. Why don't we get together for dinner tomorrow? You could come here about seven."

I nodded, relieved, too tired to carry her bags to the elevator, too tired to ride to the fourth floor. I was too tired to even feel embarrassed that I couldn't help with her bags.

She made it inside, one in each hand. A grip of steel.

My teeth were chattering as I drove home.

I ignored the flashing light on the machine, dropped my clothes on the floor, crawled into bed, and curled into a fetal position.

Butch kneaded my shoulder and Sundance pranced along my leg, both purring.

I had killed a kid and Curtis was in the hospital.

The cats were just glad I was here.

The next morning, I would have to identify the dead kid's brother. In the afternoon, I had to meet with Mike Danken and try to sort things out with some relative of the dead kid's mother. I had to see Curtis in the hospital. I had to do something about the phone messages, especially the recurring ones from my mother, as soon as I was strong enough to comfort her.

The cats fitted themselves into the angles of my body, purring.

While I was wondering how I could handle it all, I fell asleep.

Chapter
6

IN FACT, I almost overslept. I barely made it to the police station by quarter past ten the next morning. Which was all right, because everyone was running late there, too.

It was twenty till eleven by the time Matthews, the defense attorney, the assistant district attorney, and I were in the small viewing area waiting for the boys—and they were boys, all in their teens—to line up on the other side of the glass wall.

Each one was medium height, dark-haired, olive-skinned, and wearing a brown leather bomber jacket. But I recognized the one with the skittery eyes.

"Number three," I said.

"Number three, step forward," someone on the other side of the window called. Whoever it was couldn't see us, but I guess he could hear.

The Morales brother, Robert, stepped forward.

"You sure?" Matthews asked.

"Positive."

"He looks a lot like his dead brother," the defense attorney said. A short man in his early fifties with curly gray hair, wearing a baggy suit, he had been introduced as Joe Revilla. Mrs. Morales had called him because he had twice been appointed to defend Jamie. "Won't hold up in court."

"By the time we get there, the victim will have had a chance to identify him, too. In the meantime, we have enough to charge him," Cindy Griffiths, the ADA, answered.

If I'd met her on the street, I'd have sworn she was too young to be out of law school. She had a fresh face and an attitude to match.

And she thought of Curtis as "the victim." He was, of course, but it was one of those words that made me wince—nobody wants to be called "the victim"—and I wished she hadn't used it to describe someone I cared about.

"With what?" Revilla asked. "Being an accomplice at a botched robbery?"

"Come on, Joe. You know the law. His brother is dead as the result of an armed felony, and he conspired with his brother. We can charge him with second-degree murder." She seemed to enjoy the thought.

"You can't make it stick. And you couldn't even if he were an adult, which he isn't."

Cindy laughed. "Watch me."

I was, and I was feeling a little ill.

"You want some more coffee?" Matthews asked me.

I shook my head. The police station was probably the only place in town where someone could make coffee worse than my own. The cup he had given me earlier had eaten away tissue from my tongue all the way down my esophagus to my stomach, and the little that had bounced back up had eroded more tissue the second time around. Even hospital coffee would be an improvement, and I was anxious to get over there.

Matthews guided me out, all the way to the front door, something he never did.

"You did great in there," he said. "And don't mind Joe and Cindy. They do this so much, they have to make a game of it. Otherwise, they'd burn out too fast."

"Sure. I understand."

"You look a little pale. How're you holding up?"

"Okay. I asked Danken to arrange a meeting with Elva Morales."

"That might not be the best thing to do, not before Joe and Cindy work out the situation with the brother."

"I didn't mean to kill her son, and I don't want her to hate me. I can't explain, but I have to tell her that."

Matthews put his hand on my shoulder. Something about tragedy makes people think they have a right to touch you.

"You can't always make everything right. But good luck trying. If anybody can make the situation better, Mike Danken can."

I took his hand off my shoulder and shook it. Then I left.

I spent the short drive to Washoe Medical trying to catch my breath. I had decided once, after viewing a corset in a museum, that women of the nineteenth century developed a reputation for weakness and fainting because their lungs were too constricted. They simply couldn't inhale enough oxygen for their brains to function. But stress could do the same thing. I couldn't have had more trouble inhaling if an oppressive aunt had placed a foot in the middle of my back and pulled the strings around the whalebone.

And that's about how helpless I felt when I finally got in to the intensive care ward and saw Curtis lying in the bed, hooked up to the IV and the oxygen and the monitors.

I had missed Tola Rae. The nurse said she had been there earlier and would return after lunch. If I wanted, I could check the cafeteria.

Tola Rae probably had to catch her breath, too.

Intensive care is a long row of beds with curtains in between. They don't have chairs so you won't be tempted to stay too long. I leaned against the white bed and touched Curtis's hand, the one without the IV attached.

He opened his eyes and smiled, then closed them again. His fingers reached for mine. A bouncing red ball on a monitor spiked erratically when he made the gesture. I almost called for a nurse.

"Tired," he whispered, and the ball resumed its routine.

"It's okay. I can only stay a few minutes anyway. I'll come back later. We can talk later."

The faint smile lingered on his face.

I watched the red ball bounce evenly until the nurse wiggled a finger to let me know my fifteen minutes were up. I leaned over to kiss his cheek, but the ball spiked again, so I backed away, barely whispering good-bye.

The same heavyset woman with thin hair who had been sitting on the floral sofa thirty-six hours earlier was there again when I passed through the waiting room. Her eyes were shut, or I would have tried to come up with something to say to her.

I glanced inside the cafeteria and didn't see Tola Rae. I didn't blame her for taking a real break.

There were things I could have done during the two hours before I was scheduled to meet with Mike Danken. I could have tried to catch Sandra for lunch. She would have liked that, and maybe if I had watched someone else eat, I could have brought myself to try it. My business was going to hell from two days of inattention, and I could have called a couple of clients to reassure them. But I wasn't in any shape to reassure anybody. I even considered going back to bed, still trying to catch my breath.

Instead I drove to Danken's makeshift church, thinking of

how quiet and peaceful it felt inside, even with the Christmas tree. Since it was office hours, I slipped inside without knocking. I sat down in one of the folding chairs and shut my eyes.

I opened them again when I heard a woman's voice say, "You should have told me. You should have warned me she was the woman who shot Jamie."

The murmured response was too low for me to make out the words.

"You think I'm the Virgin Mary or something? How can I forgive her?"

I struggled out of the chair and took the few steps to the archway.

Mike Danken was standing in the hall with a short, heavy, dark-haired woman in a red parka. She had been about to say something more, but shut her mouth when she saw me.

"I didn't know you were here," Danken said. "Freddie O'Neal, Elena Castro."

Neither one of us held out a hand.

"I don't know about forgiveness," I said. "I'm not sure I'm asking for it, because I don't think I'm the one who did something wrong here. I'm sorry about what happened, sorry that Jamie Morales is dead. That's not the same thing as saying I did something wrong. All I'm doing here, all I'm hoping for, is that we can get past the grief and the anger and get on with our lives. If doing something for you gets us there, I'll do it if I can."

"I don't know if accepting a favor from you is any good," she said, shaking her head.

"Maybe you could both do me one," Mike said. "Since both of you arrived early, I have to think that this meeting is supposed to happen. Come to the office, and have a cup of tea, and let's discuss why Elena needs help and what Freddie could do about it."

Danken walked through a doorway without waiting to see if we would follow.

I thought about retreating to the folding chair, but I wanted the tea, and I figured he'd tell me the story if she left.

But she didn't. The office had evidently been designed as a bedroom—which couldn't have left Mike and Louise much space in the house for living quarters. The door had been taken off what would have been a closet, and bookshelves built in. Mike had taken his seat behind a large desk cluttered with papers and brochures. When I took a chair at one corner of the desk, Elena Castro took a chair at the other.

Neither of us spoke, except to thank him for the tea when he poured hot water into two mugs from the urn behind him on a credenza. The tea bags were in a wicker basket. I picked something that looked strong. Elena Castro picked one of the herbals.

"Do you want to tell her or shall I?" Danken asked.

Elena shrugged.

"Elena has been having marital problems," Danken said, learning forward across his desk. "Charlie, her husband, used to come right home from work, but for the last few weeks he has been going somewhere else on Tuesday and Thursday evenings. He refuses to tell her what is going on. When she pressed the matter last Thursday, he became physically abusive. Elena is considering ending the marriage. I thought it might help her decide, one way or the other, if she had information about what Charlie is doing two nights a week."

I glanced at Elena to see if she was embarrassed by the story. She was looking down at the pale liquid in the mug.

"A surveillance job?" I held my tone level. With effort. "Someone I care about is in the hospital, paying customers are threatening to leave me from neglect, and you're asking me to take on a pro bono surveillance job?"

"Just for one evening. Tomorrow night. If you can't take care of it in one evening, you can forget about it."

The Reverend Michael Danken, who had seemed an ordinary human being to me just the night before, had suddenly transformed himself. Sitting quietly at his desk, his square jaw had become even more prominent, and he had somehow assumed one of those charismatic faces that held your attention, one of those charismatic voices that promised unconditional love, love even if you said no, so much love that you couldn't possibly say no to the one little thing he was asking in a couple of short sentences.

"Considering my current notoriety, I don't think I'm the best choice for surveillance," I grumbled.

"Perhaps not. But you're the choice we have."

I felt annoyed and manipulated, but I agreed to give Elena Castro one evening of my life.

"Do you have a picture of Charlie?" I asked.

"Not with me. I'll leave one here tomorrow morning. You can pick it up."

Elena didn't sound grateful, which further annoyed me.

"Good. You can also leave information on where he works, what kind of car he drives, and what he was wearing when he left the house. I'll return everything here Friday morning, along with a report on what I find." I didn't bother to add that she could pick it up.

"Thank you for your help," she said to Danken. "I hope this works. And thank you for the tea. I will see you tomorrow."

She put down the mug and walked out. I almost did the same.

"If that's the cousin, I guess Matthews was right," I said.

"There's no point in trying to talk with Jamie Morales's mother."

"Well, not yet. He's probably right about that. But this action will keep the line of communication open, and I think that's what you really want to do."

I wasn't certain what I really wanted to do, so I didn't say anything. The tea was warm and bitter, and I decided I wanted to finish it.

"Do you have some kind of official connection with the police department?" I asked.

"No. But I was a police officer for twenty years, before I became a minister, and sometimes that helps when you want to inspire trust."

"You don't look that old." Even as I said it, I started looking for the small lines at the corners of the eyes, the hint of sag at the corners of the jaw. I found them, but not without a search.

"I used to feel that old." Danken smiled, deepening the crinkles. "I've been getting younger for the past six years. I offer the secret to anyone who asks. Not that you need to look or feel younger."

"For two days now I've been feeling older than my mother looks." When he waited, expectantly, I added, "Sorry. That would only be a joke if you knew my mother."

He nodded and waited.

"You can't really want to hear about my relationship with my mother," I said.

"I'd love to hear about your relationship with your mother. I'm sure she must be a very unusual woman, or you wouldn't be the special human being sitting here with me."

Danken sat there as calmly as he had been sitting the night in the hospital, when he had admitted he didn't know all the answers, but was more than willing to hear all the questions. I still wasn't interested in that level of intimacy.

"Another time," I said, putting down my mug.

"I hope you mean that," Danken answered. "I'll be here if you do."

I stood up and held out my hand.

"I'll keep that in mind."

He stood too, clasping my hand in both of his, clasping my eyes as well. "I want you to know that I'm praying for your friend Curtis. And you. Prayers aren't always answered the way we think they ought to be, but I have a good feeling about this one. I think you and Curtis have a lot of life ahead. Together."

"You're way ahead of me, Reverend." I extricated my hand. "Way ahead of me. But I'm sure Curtis won't mind your prayers."

Danken let me go with a smile.

I was feeling better enough that I stopped for take-out chicken before going home.

Butch and Sundance ended up getting more than I did. I ate the coleslaw and the biscuit and tried to make sense out of what was going on.

I gave up on that pretty quickly. Instead, I spent the afternoon calling the few clients I had and returning the calls from the possible ones on my answering machine, letting them know I couldn't do anything for a day or two. Once I got started, talking wasn't as hard as I had feared. Everybody had heard the news and seemed to feel that hiring me had been such a good choice that I was worth waiting for.

But I couldn't help thinking there was something wrong about a killing being good for business.

I had to drop that thought when it was time to take a shower and get ready to have dinner with Tola Rae. And it wasn't easy to do. I was reminded of the double shooting every time I circled around the place on the carpet where I had discarded my bloodstained clothes. I was reminded when I had to put on my sheepskin jacket, too heavy for the evening, because my blue denim one was gone, and my white denim one had a coffee stain that wouldn't come out.

I was reminded again when I parked the Jeep, when I rode up in the elevator, knowing that Tola Rae was going to answer my ring because Curtis was in the hospital.

When she opened the door, we stared at each other. It took her a beat to remember to invite me in.

"If you don't mind, I'd just as soon not," I answered. "Once I sit down, it's hard to get going again. I'd like to conserve energy until we get to the restaurant."

"I understand," she said. "I'll get my coat."

I stood in the hall for the moment it took her to put on the short fur jacket. I wondered if she also understood that I didn't want to go in while she was staying there. I didn't quite understand it myself, but I didn't feel comfortable at the thought of being in Curtis's apartment while Curtis's mother was in residence.

Tola Rae was from another culture and another genera-tion, and I couldn't help wondering as well if she disap-proved of me by definition, simply because I was sleeping with her son.

Besides, we had decorated his apartment together. I hadn't put up a Christmas tree at home—I never do—but I had helped select and decorate his. And I didn't want to see it just then.

I couldn't come up with a good suggestion for dinner, so we ended up at the Comstock Room of the Mother Lode by default. It's as swank as a nineteenth-century bordello, all red velvet wallpaper dotted with cloudy sconces casting dim light on the patrons. The restaurant is on the seventh floor of the casino, and it used to have quite a view. Now about all you can see is the neon signs from other casinos.

At least nobody there had gotten carried away by Christmas. One garland around the reservation desk was all I saw.

When we got off the elevator, Tola Rae looked around as if it matched her expectations perfectly.

A hostess dressed to fit the design theme showed us to a table and offered to bring us drinks. Tola Rae asked for a wine list. She held it close to the flickering gas lamp and put on half glasses to read it.

"Do you know what you're ordering for dinner?" she asked.

"Pick the wine you want. I'm having a beer," I replied. I knew it wasn't the answer she wanted. I couldn't help her out.

"Curtis likes you," she said, peering at me over the rim of her glasses. "I'm trying very hard to do the same."

"I didn't mean to sound rude. If Curtis were here, this would be a lot easier. I'm not very good at small talk."

"Curtis probably thinks I'm too good at it."

"He's never said that. And he has talked about you."

"I won't ask what he said. Nor will I counter with what he's said about you. We'll simply talk about him."

Discussing Curtis got us through dinner. He turned out to be the only common ground we could come up with, but since Tola Rae did indeed have a talent for small talk, one piece of common ground was enough. Especially once she realized that I hate baby stories. Under other circumstances I might not have been quite as fascinated with the tales about Curtis spraining his knee playing prep school basketball, or Curtis causing a fender-bender in the family car a week after he got his driver's license. Then again, I might have been. Somehow she made them almost charming. And not baby stories.

Her charm was showing little signs of strain by the time we finished the meal. Still, neither of us wanted coffee, and I was relieved when the evening was over, when I could, without being rude, drop her off at Curtis's apartment building and plead exhaustion as an excuse not to come in.

In truth, I was exhausted. And all I had done was eat dinner with a woman I didn't know and smile at appropriate intervals. I wondered how she held up.

The calls from reporters had dwindled to the point where I didn't dread playing back messages. But I was bothered by Baxter Cate, the man who had an undisclosed idea of mutual benefit. He had left another message. I might have to call him back to get rid of him. In the morning.

I did call the hospital for one last report on Curtis's condition. The nurse said he was doing so well that they planned to move him out of intensive care the next day. On that news, I decided I could go to sleep.

Once in bed, I turned on the television, not because I really wanted to watch anything, but out of habit, and because I knew both cats would land like boulders on the blanket once they had finished eating. I might as well wait for them to settle.

I channel-surfed my way to a middle-aged John Wayne wearing a badge and a smile, holding a rifle in one hand and a pistol in the other, asking five men to surrender. When they refused, he shot them all, killing two, still smiling.

John Wayne, the actor who missed World War II, who probably never really shot a man in his life, playing a smiling stone killer on the side of the law. I hadn't seen him that way before, and he was suddenly ugly to me. I turned the set off.

Sleeping wasn't as easy as I thought it was going to be.

That night I dreamed about Alan Ladd, in buckskin, with blood running down his arm. He was looking at me with sadness, saying that killing brands you, even killing done in a good cause.

I heard myself calling, "Shane, come back," as he faded away.

Chapter
7

THE MORNING WAS so bright and clear that I decided to walk to Washoe Medical. Taking deep breaths of crisp air had to be good for the spirit.

Better for the spirit was getting there and finding that Curtis had already been transferred to a regular room. The woman at the information desk gave me directions. I rode the elevator to the third floor, made a wrong turn, but found it.

He was in the second bed, close to the window.

I stepped past the first bed as quietly as anyone in boots can step and peered around the curtain.

He was still hooked to an IV and a monitor, with a split tube feeding oxygen to his nostrils, but his eyes were open, and he smiled when he saw me.

I smiled back, determined to be undaunted by Tola Rae, who had been looking out the window until Curtis whispered, "Hi."

I said "Hi" to Curtis and "Good morning" to Tola Rae and then stood there, not sure how to proceed.

Tola Rae came through again.

"I'd like a cup of coffee," she said. "Could I bring either of you anything?"

"Not for me, thanks," I said.

Curtis shook his head and whispered, "Thanks."

"How are you?" I asked, once Tola Rae had picked up her purse and left.

"Lung hurts when I breathe. And when I don't. Tired. Otherwise okay. You?"

I thought I could say fine and carry it off. But I looked at him lying there, looked at the tubes and machines, and nothing came out. I felt my face twist and I tried to hold it in place.

He held out the hand that wasn't attached to anything.

"I love you, Little Sureshot," he said.

I sat on the edge of the bed, grabbed his hand, and held it against my cheek.

"I'm so sorry." The words became a strangled sob.

"For saving my life?"

"I didn't save your life. He wouldn't have shot again. From the angle I hit him, he had to be turning away. If I hadn't shot him, he would have escaped." Tears started, so rapidly they almost blinded me, and I had to stop for sight and breath.

Curtis waited until I was calm enough to hear.

"That isn't the way the witnesses told the story. Tola Rae summarized the newspapers for me, and two witnesses said you shot in self-defense. The little I've seen on television left the same impression."

"I wouldn't have caught him on the side of the head."

"You did the right thing," he whispered. "I believe that. What did Deke say?"

"He thinks I did the right thing. But I didn't tell him the kid had to have been turning."

Curtis raised his eyebrows. "Tell him. He'll still say you did the right thing. And Matthews?"

"He thinks I did the right thing. But the coroner hasn't made any kind of report to say the kid was turning away."

Curtis blinked and gave kind of a half nod. "Maybe he wasn't. You did what anyone would have done."

"Anyone with a gun in her boot."

"Are you having some kind of crisis of conscience? A dark night of the soul?" He tugged at my hand, and I put my head on his shoulder. His neck had an unfamiliar medicinal smell.

"I think so. And I hate it."

"What doesn't kill us, makes us stronger."

"That's what your mother said."

"If I'd known that, I would have said something else."

I had to laugh. "She's easier to get along with than I thought she'd be."

"Other people's mothers always are."

"Yeah, but she actually seems to be making the situation better. That's a valuable talent, one that not all mothers have."

"Yes. And I am grateful for that." He started to say something more, but it was cut off by a coughing spasm.

I jerked upright. He grabbed for a tissue from the box on his bedside tray and spit some pink liquid into it.

"Are you okay? Should I call the nurse?"

He took a sip of water. "Okay. I'll be glad when it doesn't hurt anymore."

"Do you know how long? Can anybody tell you how long this is going to take?"

He shook his head, then leaned back and closed his eyes. I sat there in silence, holding his hand again, until Tola Rae came back with her coffee.

I started to slip my hand away, but Curtis grasped hold, then opened his eyes.

"I ought to go," I said.

"Where?" he asked.

"Just down the street to a tiny church. The minister there thinks I ought to help out the less fortunate. I said I'd stop by this morning."

"Danken?"

"He was in to see you, right?"

Curtis nodded. "Seemed okay."

"Yeah, I guess so."

"I would describe him as better than okay," Tola Rae interjected. "I thought he was quite personable, not too pushy, and sincerely hopeful that he could be of service."

"He's probably all of that," I said. "I'll come back here later."

Curtis dropped my hand and made a gesture of blessing. He must have known I was getting restless and edgy in the hospital half-room, that Tola Rae's return made it seem suddenly cramped. "See you then."

She was easier to get along with than I had feared, but we were still in the small-talk stage, and I couldn't sit quietly and listen to her stories right then. Maybe she and I would reach a level of ease with one another. In the meantime, I had to ration the amount of time I spent with her.

Tola Rae and I exchanged polite good-byes.

I made a fast escape down the elevator, past the front desk and the tree and the piano, and out the front door.

The high, hot sun startled me. The main entrance to Washoe Medical is at the top of a circular, curving ramp, opposite the entrance to the parking lot. A pair of wooden benches mark the edges of a concrete rest area, a place to eat or to regather energy—not a place to smoke, the sign warns about that—for the healers or the friends of those in need of healing.

I was dizzy for a moment, and almost sat down, but I decided my body was complaining about the lack of food. I hadn't eaten since dinner with Tola Rae the night before. I had to think about eating soon. After I picked up the picture of Charlie Castro from Mike Danken.

I walked across the grassy triangle known as Pickett Park to Ryland, then crossed the corner to Danken's combination house and church.

He was sitting on the front steps, a large envelope in his hands. He waited until I sat beside him, then handed it to me.

"You've seen Curtis?" he asked.

"Yeah. He's doing better. He said you'd stopped by. That was nice of you."

"Happy to do it."

I opened the envelope and took out a framed, eight-by-ten wedding picture. The woman in the bridal veil and radiant smile was Elena Castro. The man in the tux standing next to her was smiling, too, but the smile was all teeth and no heart. His dark eyes were focused somewhere to the side of the camera.

I've heard that sometimes with wedding pictures the couple has to make a choice between which of them is going to look good, because the photographer didn't catch them both at their best in the same shot. This had to have been the shot of her. He didn't look unattractive—the curly hair and thin moustache could have belonged to a matinee idol—so much as untrustworthy.

I wondered if Elena had intentionally wanted me to see this one, hoping it would influence my opinion of her husband. I decided to reserve judgment on him.

"Is he still wearing the tux?" I asked.

"Not this morning. He was wearing his uniform when he left the house. Charlie is a delivery man for Sierra Express Parcel Service."

"Wait. He delivers packages for Sierra Express, which contracts to make deliveries with local department stores and appliance stores and places like that, and this is less than a week before Christmas, and his wife is worried about late evenings at work?"

Danken beamed at me. "I told you it was a simple problem."

"It's a waste of time. But I said I'd do it. What time does she think he should turn his truck in, and what kind of car does he drive?"

"His shift is supposed to end at four-thirty, and he drives a Honda that Elena described as rust-colored. Do you know where the Sierra Express facilities are?"

"On Valley Road?"

He nodded. "What else do you need?"

"A clear conscience, and I hope this does it."

Danken frowned. I hadn't seen him frown before. The expression didn't fit his face very well, and I felt uncomfortable for having caused it.

"I wish I could promise you that," he said.

"I'm not asking you."

"No, you're really asking God."

I hadn't quite looked at it that way, and I wasn't sure I wanted to.

"I haven't asked about your religious beliefs," he continued. "And I don't want to force mine on you. But I do believe that God has a master plan for all of us, and that everything, even apparent evil—and I don't think what you did was evil, I think you did what you had to do under the circumstances—I believe that all events ultimately testify to God's goodness. I don't know God's will in this. I may never know what He has in mind. Still, I have prayed for guidance, and I think we are on the right track. Sooner or later the act that will clear your conscience, insofar as it needs clearing, will occur to one of us."

"I didn't know we were in this together," I said.

"I think we are," he answered. "I think we are. I don't want you to feel that you're out there alone."

That was more togetherness than I could handle. I stood up and held out my hand.

"I'll check out Charlie Castro tonight," I said, "and I'll let you know tomorrow how well I've slept."

"Fine." Danken was smiling again as he stood. He clasped my hand in both of his. "I'll be here."

"And you can give Elena Castro back her picture in the meantime. I think I can spot him without it."

Danken chuckled as he took the envelope. I felt his eyes watching me as I walked away. I didn't look back.

I stopped for a hamburger and coffee at a fast-food joint on Wells Avenue. I had intended to take them home with me, but I was too hungry. I sat down at a table, ripped the bag apart, and bit into a very sloppy, oversauced concoction. I hoped it was a good sign, that I was getting hungry again. Probably all it meant was that I wasn't quite as worried about Curtis anymore.

The sandwich was greasy, and I ate it too quickly, and it clotted in my stomach, the lump getting heavier as I walked. I should have had chicken soup. But Curtis was the injured one—I wasn't—and I felt angry that I hadn't rebounded to some kind of normal sense of self in the couple of days since the shooting.

Angry or not, I couldn't push myself to do much more than check messages when I got home. I was down to one persistent tabloid reporter and Baxter Cate, who kept saying his name as if it might mean something to me. It didn't. And of course Ramona had called.

I spent the next few hours answering e-mail and playing Tetris. There was no one I wanted to talk to.

By four the sky was beginning to turn indigo, and I took my sheepskin coat when I left for the Sierra Express office. I wasn't expecting much of a surveillance, but the air cools quickly once the sun is down.

Valley Road began just north of the railroad tracks and ran through what appeared to be one junk heap after another—lumber, scrap metal, auto body work, what have you. The address I wanted was about a block and a half shy of Interstate 80, a relatively new, almost clean building in the midst of a large parking lot.

There was no place to park the Jeep except the lot. The street was narrow, the lot was fenced, and there was nothing that could be called a curb or a sidewalk. After considering the combination of narrow street and wide trucks, I drove through the open gate and pulled into a marked space next to a red Toyota, as far from the front door as was available.

Several of the white trucks with the blue stylized mountains of the Sierra Express logo were already parked at the side of the building, and two more drove in as I was getting settled. It was already too dark to see their drivers. I got out to look for a rust-colored Honda.

A Honda that could easily have been called rust-colored, and dented, was parked behind the building, one of only four against the chain link fence that divided this lot from something that loomed heavy and hulking in the deep twilight on a lot that extended to Elko Avenue. Since the sole exit was the driveway I had used to enter, I returned to the Jeep.

I waited there in the cold while three of the four cars left. Shortly after, the lights went out in the office. The floodlights at the corners of the lot were too dim to do much good. I got out to catch whoever was locking the building, apparently the owner of the red Toyota.

She turned when she heard my boots. She took one look at my face and screamed.

"Don't shoot!"

"No gun," I said, holding my hands wide, palms facing her. My gut had knotted. I had a sudden flash of Jamie Morales lying dead and bloody in a dimly lit parking lot. I grabbed a breath and kept going. "I was looking for Charlie Castro. What time are you expecting him?"

"Charlie?"

I wished for a brighter light so that I could have a chance at deciphering the emotions running across her face. She was nineteen tops, with long, dark hair and skin the color of cocoa after the whipped cream was stirred in.

"Charlie," I repeated.

"He didn't come to work today," she said. "Maybe you could come back tomorrow."

"If he didn't come to work, why is his car here?"

"It isn't—it couldn't be."

"It is. In back. Are there more lights you can turn on?"

I had my flashlight in the Jeep, but I didn't want to walk away from her.

"No. Just what's on already," she said.

"Then I'm going to ask you to come with me to my car, where I'm going to get a flashlight, and we're going to walk together around the building to Charlie's car, okay?"

She nodded, but she looked as frozen as a jackrabbit about to be road kill. I grabbed her arm and she screamed again.

"Quit that," I said. "What are you screaming about?"

"You killed Jamie. You killed Jamie. I saw you on

television, saying you were right to kill him. Why are you here?"

I could feel her whole body trembling. I dropped her arm.

"Oh, hell. Not to hurt you. And I'm sorry about Jamie, but he shot first."

"I don't have a gun," she said, starting to sob.

"I don't either." I didn't have one in my hand, anyway. Just in my boot. "Now come with me."

I took her arm again, and this time she let me drag her to the Jeep. She stood there whimpering while I got the flashlight.

"We're going to walk around the building to Charlie's car," I said. "Can you do that?"

She just whimpered, so I grasped her elbow and pulled.

Charlie's rust-colored Honda was still parked facing the chain link fence. The sight of it startled her into some kind of awareness that maybe I wasn't planning to kill her.

She shook my hand away and walked by herself toward the car.

"But he didn't check in this morning," she said. "I had to call a substitute. Nobody answered at his house."

I turned the flashlight beam first into the front seat, then into the back. Nothing.

"Which truck was his? Do you know?"

"Number three," she replied. "The third one from the fence. But somebody else drove it today."

I swung the flashlight toward the trucks, then let the beam fall back.

At another angle, I might have missed the blood.

There were only a few drops on the bumper of the Honda and a few drops to the right of the trunk lid. If I hadn't been already thinking about blood, I might have thought they were motor oil, or even paint splatters, because they were so close to the color of the car.

"I'm going to force the trunk," I told her, pulling a small knife out of my pocket.

"You can't do that," she said, stepping back.

"I know, but I can't wait for the police, either."

I jammed the narrow blade into the lock and twisted.

When the lock gave and I used the knife to lever the lid open, she started screaming again. This time I didn't try to stop her.

Chapter
8

WHEN HE SAW the corpse, Matthews wasn't happy.

I had known he wouldn't be, but I couldn't help that. I did the best I could.

I left the knife blade in the lock and used the handle to ease the trunk lid back down. I didn't touch anything with my hands.

Once she couldn't see the body, Letty Rashad stopped screaming.

Not that she told me her name, or that I even asked for it. I didn't know it until after she gave her statement to Michelle Urrutia, the officer who drove Matthews to the parking lot.

I dragged Letty back to the front of the building and waited while she unlocked the door and turned on the lights. I didn't like leaving the corpse with no one to watch it, but I was reasonably certain that Letty and I were alone, and that I could spot any newcomer before the crime scene was interfered with. Any more than I had already interfered, that is.

I told her the number of the direct line to Homicide and stood in the doorway while she talked. She said more than she needed to—including the information that I had forced the trunk—but I didn't try to stop her.

Matthews and Urrutia were there in five minutes.

I was still in the doorway. Letty was cowering behind her desk. Neither of us had attempted to start a conversation. She was dealing with the shock of seeing Charlie Castro's body. I was dealing with the shock of having an identity as the woman who shot Jamie Morales.

"You should have called first," Matthews sighed as he got out of the car.

"For a couple of drops of what might have been motor oil? Or blood from a cut finger? If the trunk had been empty, I would have apologized to both Charlie and Elena Castro and paid for the lock. But if I had called you before opening it, you would have called Elena. You couldn't open the trunk without her and without a warrant. I would have waited for you. You would have waited for her. The whole process would have taken all night. And it might have been for nothing if Charlie Castro had left the car here yesterday and Elena forgot to tell me."

I exchanged greetings with Michelle Urrutia and got out of her way so she could reach Letty and the desk. Matthews and I walked around the building to the car.

"How did you get involved?" Matthews asked. "Is this a case?"

"No. I have no client here. Or at least I'm not being paid, so I don't see it as having a client. Mike Danken thought it would be a good idea if I did a favor for a woman with a simple problem. Make everybody feel better. Now one of us has to tell her that it wasn't so simple after all."

"The guy's wife?"

"Yeah. Elena Castro. She wanted to know where he was spending his evenings. Danken and I both figured it was

Christmas overtime. Dead in the trunk of his car wasn't an answer that occurred to either of us."

I used the knife to flip the trunk lid open again. Matthews closed his eyes.

"I wish I hadn't seen that."

"Sorry. I didn't touch anything else. I didn't even check for a neck pulse once I saw the hole behind his ear."

"Just as well. Heads don't normally turn that far. Somebody may have broken his neck shoving him in."

Matthews had been leaning closer, shining his flashlight into various shadows. Castro's body was in a fetal position with the head turned up, eyes staring vacantly past his left shoulder, mouth gaping open. The angle of his chin had bothered me the first time. Now it struck me as grotesque.

But that wasn't the worst of it. The worst of it was that someone had stuck white chicken feathers all over his face, using a dark material as glue.

I was standing where Castro's line of vision should have been. I took a step back and turned away.

"I don't suppose you can tell if that's tar," I said.

"Not without an analysis. But it would go with the feathers, if not with a bullet hole and a broken neck. Somebody wanted to make sure he was both humiliated and dead. We'll have to wait for the ME to know any more than that." He snapped off the flashlight. "So what else have you got to tell me?"

"I got here around four-twenty, parked in front, and waited for the car to pass on its way out. When the building was closing and it hadn't come by, I dragged whoever she is from the office around to check it out with me. That's all I know."

"Why'd the wife want him tailed? Why did she think it wasn't just some kind of Christmas overtime?"

"Now that you're asking, it's because he became physically abusive—Mike Danken's words—when she asked where he was going on Tuesday and Thursday nights."

"And you didn't get excited hearing some woman got beat up by her husband?" He snapped the flashlight on again and started walking around the car.

"She looked okay to me and I had other things on my mind. I guess I made a mistake."

"Tuesdays and Thursdays. How many weeks?" Matthews eased himself onto his knees and peered under the car.

"I don't know."

He got back to his feet in stages, brushing off his pants on the way.

"Do you know why Mike Danken chose this particular good deed for you to do?"

"Danken told me that Elena Castro is Elva Morales's cousin. He wanted to make everybody feel better."

"Yeah, okay, sometimes Mike makes a mistake, too."

Three cars pulled around the building, saving us from further conversation. I recognized the ME and the police photographer. I didn't know the others.

"Do you need me?" I asked.

"Go home," Matthews said. "We'll talk tomorrow."

The ME and the photographer were getting ready to go to work, so I didn't stop to say hello.

I did take a short detour to the office, to let Michelle Urrutia know I was leaving.

"Take care," she said. "And lock yourself in your bedroom till after Christmas, will you? I don't need the overtime."

I smiled. Michelle's okay, and I didn't want to snap at her, even though the line wasn't funny.

Letty Rashad glared at both of us.

"I want to go home," she said.

"And you can do that soon," Michelle told her. "As soon

as I'm certain Detective Matthews doesn't want to talk to you."

The office was bright and warm. The contrast with the parking lot, as I stepped back out into it, shook me.

Letty Rashad may have wanted to go home, but I didn't.

I wasn't ready to be alone with the cats.

And I couldn't go to Washoe Medical, because I didn't want to tell Curtis and Tola Rae what had happened.

I drove the few blocks west on Second Street, turned north on Center, and pulled in to the Mother Lode's parking garage. I was so anxious to get to the coffee shop that I almost hit a Saturn pulling out of a space. I backed up before the couple in the front seat noticed. I took the spot once they'd maneuvered around to the exit lane.

I jogged across the alley, rudely pushed my way past the tourists dawdling in the aisle between the slots and the roulette tables, and passed four people who were simply riding up the escalator.

I didn't stop until I realized that Deke wasn't in the coffee shop. His stool at the counter was vacant.

Diane waved at me, so I went ahead to my usual place next to Deke's.

"You're early," she said. "Sit down and I'll bring you a beer."

"Early?"

"Didn't you check the time? Deke won't be here for another hour or so."

"Oh. I guess I didn't check the time." I settled onto the stool. "Sure. Bring me a beer."

I picked up a Keno ticket and a marker.

I had never felt less lucky in my life.

I replaced them both in the holder.

I had drunk about half the beer and demolished about half

the label with my fingernail when I felt Deke easing his bulk onto the stool next to me.

"So what's going on?" he asked.

"What do you mean?"

"Diane took a potty break to call me and tell me to get over here. That's what I mean. So what's going on?"

"Did you ever have a time in your life when nothing was going right?"

"One or two. How's Curtis?"

"Still in the hospital with tubes in him."

"He's alive. That's one thing going right."

"I thought you didn't much like him."

"That don't matter. You do."

"Okay. I'll give you that. One thing's going right. Sort of. Even that one could be better—he could never have been shot."

"You ordered yet?" When I shook my head, Deke called to Diane. "We'll eat."

"The good deed Danken wanted me to do, following the Morales cousin's husband . . ."

"I remember. What happened?"

"I found him dead in the trunk of his car."

"Shit."

"Yeah, that's what Matthews said, too."

Diane must have put in the order when she saw Deke walk past the cashier, because my hamburger and his steak appeared almost as if by magic.

"How did he die?"

"Not sure. Bullet hole, broken neck. And something else that looks like it could be tar and feathers."

"Tar and feathers?"

"Just on his face, as far as I could see. Matthews said he had to wait for the medical examiner before he could say anything more."

"What did Danken say?" Deke asked around a mouthful of rare meat.

"I haven't talked to him." I dumped a pool of ketchup on my plate. I wasn't certain how hungry I was, especially for a second hamburger so close to the first, but I could at least eat a couple of fries.

"Best you do that."

"He'll feel bad. I don't want to deal with him feeling bad."

"You don't have to deal with him feeling bad, but you better deal with you feeling bad. Avoiding Danken won't help you feel better."

"Telling him won't either. But I'll call him when I get home. And Ramona. It'll piss her off too much to hear about it on the news."

"And Curtis?"

That one was tougher. I put off answering until I had swallowed. "I think he has to wait until tomorrow. He'll probably be asleep anyway."

"He won't be pissed like Ramona if he finds out from the television. But he might not be happy if he thinks you think he's so weak you have to protect him from bad news."

"I don't think he's weak." I smeared a little ketchup on the top half of the hamburger bun, stuck the whole thing together with the tomato slice and the lettuce leaf, and cut it in half. I figured I could handle half. "I think he has to conserve his strength, though. Besides, his mother's there. I like Tola Rae, but I'm not sure how she feels about my profession."

"I suspect you are about to find out."

"Yeah, me too."

I knew from what Curtis had told me that Tola Rae was a strong woman, gutsy in her own way. She had been born into wealth and raised in the tradition of noblesse oblige — she believed she had a responsibility to those who weren't quite so lucky. And then she had married well—Curtis's father, Cabell Breckinridge, had been a distant relative of John Cabell Breckinridge, a former vice president of the United States who defected to the Confederacy, although that's not exactly the way Curtis described it.

John C. Breckinridge and his immediate descendants had stayed in Kentucky, and at least one cousin had ended up settling in Virginia, but they all would have fit right into the Nevada of the late nineteenth century. Nevada had joined the Union in 1864 as a free state, opposed to states' rights, over the objections of the many Confederate sympathizers who had crossed the desert in search of gold before the war. Ironically, the states' rights crowd eventually prevailed, to the point that by the late twentieth century, even the counties were arguing for the right to secede from the authority of the federal government—not because of slavery, but because of federal overprotection of the environment. Abraham Lincoln would have had his hands full with that crowd.

Cabell Breckinridge had died of a heart attack while Curtis was at Princeton. The widowed Tola Rae could have spent the rest of her life at the country club. Instead, she had made helping a private foundation that was dedicated to providing teenaged mothers with the skills to get off welfare her personal cause.

Curtis had told me enough stories about her that I knew she had never backed off from the courage of her convictions, even when they took her to lousy neighborhoods where she had to confront angry parents.

I wasn't certain yet what any of that would mean on a personal level. She might respect me, even like me, and still want me out of her son's life because I wouldn't fit in with the country club crowd. Her opinion wouldn't sway him, though, if he weren't lying in a hospital bed with Tola Rae standing guard. But he was.

"Is it because his great-grandparents owned slaves?" I asked.

"Come again?"

"Is that why you don't much like Curtis?"

"I hadn't thought to dislike him for that. But I might, now that you've mentioned it."

"Then why?"

Deke regarded me through black, red, and yellow eyes that could have passed for shooting marbles. I had to pick up my hamburger.

"He thinks he's better than other people because he works when he doesn't have to. He thinks he's still some kind of lord of the plantation. And when he talks to me, which he only does because he likes you, he pretends to be just folks when deep in his heart he knows he isn't. That's why. You want a beer?"

I nodded, and he waved at Diane.

"I don't think Curtis could just retire," I said. "You're right, he thinks people ought to work, so he does it himself. And he thinks they should want to, as well. That's why he studies leadership, because he wants to figure out how to make that happen."

"Better than the old whip, I guess."

"Stop that. Besides, Curtis doesn't stand to inherit so much that he could drop everything and be an international playboy. He has to do something."

"Good to know he really is just folks."

"He does respect you, I know that. And he sounds condescending sometimes when he doesn't mean to."

"Just that old echo of the way his grandpappy used to talk to my grandpappy."

"I've been in his apartment. There aren't any Stars and

Bars hanging on the walls, and the doorbell doesn't play 'Dixie.'"

"It don't matter. I'm not going to take to him, and he isn't going to take to me. But that doesn't mean the two of you can't take to each other."

Diane brought my beer and smiled at us. I thanked her, Deke nodded.

"Okay," I said. "Okay. But you ought to know—I told him, I think the kid may have been turning away when I shot. And the first thing he said was that I ought to tell you."

Deke had to struggle for a moment with the knowledge that I had told Curtis first.

"He was there," I added.

"So he thinks I may be a little more objective, maybe. I guess your friend Curtis still thinks it was a good shot, no matter which way the delinquent was headed."

"He does."

"Then he and I finally agree about something. You may remember that I once taught survival skills to young Air Force recruits. I would have flunked out any one of those poor pitiful nineteen-year-olds who didn't have the guts to shoot to kill once a buddy was down. Flunked him out and sent him home with his tail between his legs."

I did remember that. A stint in survival training at what used to be Stead Air Force Base but was now the Truckee Meadows Community College had brought Deke to Reno a couple of decades earlier. I had never figured out why he stayed.

"That was about war."

"When somebody shoots at you, it's always about war."

I had to think about that. Deke let me brood in silence through the rest of dinner. I finished my hamburger. He finished his steak and a piece of apple pie as well. If I thought it was any of my business, I'd tell him that at his age, he ought to worry about his weight gain. But it isn't, so I don't.

I said good-bye, paid my check, and left.

When I got home, I was surprised at how early it was.

The only messages were three from reporters, including one from Mark Martin.

I had no excuse to avoid Ramona.

I sat down at my desk, picked up the phone, and punched out her number. Sundance hopped up on my lap and batted the cord. He has a psychic connection with my mother that I've given up trying to figure out.

"I'm not exactly going to be on the news," I said when she answered. Sundance settled down and began to purr. I rubbed his ears with my free hand. "But I might be mentioned. I was asked to do a surveillance job, as a favor to someone. The subject was dead before I got to him."

"You found another dead body? Is that what you're saying?"

I wanted to ask what she meant by "another," but Ramona has a long memory, and I was afraid she'd tell me.

"I found a corpse. Yes. And nobody may care who found it by the time the story is on the late news. In case somebody does care, however, I thought you would want to know in advance."

She sighed, a very long sigh. "That was thoughtful of you. I appreciate your thoughtfulness."

"And you would appreciate it even more if I didn't have to be thoughtful about finding a corpse. I know. And I don't want to hear it right now." I had cut her off, and I fought off feeling guilty for being rude. Sundance stopped purring and dug his claws into my knee. I pushed him off my lap.

Ramona waited to make certain I was finished, then came back more quietly. "Well, of course. You're upset, and I don't blame you. About your work, and about Curtis, too. Have you seen him?"

"Earlier today. He was doing a lot better. His mother's here, and she told them to treat me like family."

"I know. I called Washoe Medical for a progress report, and when they put me through to the room, she answered the phone. She seems like a very nice person. I hope I can meet her while she's here."

"I'm sure she'll want to meet you, too. As soon as she decides she doesn't have to spend the day at Curtis's bedside."

"Why don't you ask her to come up here with you for Christmas dinner?"

I struggled with the whole idea of Christmas dinner.

"I'll let her know you asked."

I wormed my way off the phone as politely as I could. The short conversation had sapped the little bit of energy I had picked up talking with Deke.

And I still had the Reverend Danken to go.

Louise Danken answered the phone with such cheer in her voice that I cringed as I asked to speak with Mike.

"Freddie!" he exclaimed when he picked up the receiver. "How did it go?"

"Not well. Charlie Castro's dead. Execution-style hit. Sort of, anyway. I found him in the trunk of his car in the Sierra Express parking lot. He never made it to work in the morning, so whoever got him must have driven the car there, and must have wanted him found soon."

I got all that out on one breath. Then I shut my eyes and waited for his response.

"I'm so sorry." He barely paused before he said it. "This is my fault—I didn't take Elena as seriously as I should have. What a terrible experience that must have been for you. Are you all right?"

I hate that question, especially when I'm not sure of the answer. I particularly hated it because Matthews had suggested maybe I hadn't taken Elena as seriously as I should have.

"I'm okay. Matthews has the case. He'll be able to tell you more once he hears from the ME and once he sifts through the list of people who had reasons to be in the parking lot. Maybe someone saw Castro's car with another driver."

"You haven't talked to Elena, have you?"

"No."

"I'm sorry, of course you haven't. And you sound tired. I should let you get some rest. I'll call Roy in the morning."

"Okay. And thanks for trying to help."

The silence was long enough that I knew I'd made a mistake.

"I'll come up with something better," he said at last. "That's a promise."

"No, listen, you don't have to. I'm not asking you for anything. And I really meant the thank you."

"I know that, Freddie. But it's still a promise. I'll talk with you soon."

I hung up the phone and put my head down on the desk, too tired to move. I jerked upright when the phone rang again. My hand was still on the receiver, and I pulled it to my ear.

"Is this Freddie O'Neal?"

I recognized the voice. It was Baxter Cate, the man who had left the message about a proposition of mutual value.

"Tell me," I said. "But make it fast."

"Now, now, Miss O'Neal. I'm a businessman, and I don't do business over the phone. Could we arrange a meeting?"

"Not unless you tell me what this is about and I like the idea."

"This is about values. This is about the firm conviction that robbing a human being at gunpoint is wrong, and nothing can make it right."

"I need more than that."

"What if I told you that I wanted to set up a series of school assemblies around the state of Nevada, send you on a speaking tour to explain to young people what happened, and why it happened, and why what that boy did was wrong?"

"I'd tell you I'm not the right person for the job. I'd also ask what you get out of it."

"I think you are the right person for the job. What I get out of it will depend on how effective you are. I left my name on your answering machine—Baxter Cate. I own Liberty Gun Works, you may have heard of it."

"Oh, hell. You think I'll scare people into buying guns. I'm the wrong person and I'm not interested."

"You could scare them into buying guns, or you could scare them out of committing robberies. Your choice."

"Forget it."

I hung up before he could say anything more.

Some kind of muck had oozed through the phone line as I talked to him. I had to take a shower before I went to bed.

I turned on the late news, hoping I wouldn't be mentioned. But Mark Martin had interviewed Letty Rashad, who looked a lot better on camera than I had. He summarized at the end.

"We haven't talked to Freddie O'Neal yet, but her discovery of the dead body of Charlie Castro, right on the heels of shooting his wife's cousin's son—which was ruled justifiable by the District Attorney's office—can't be a coincidence. Back to you, Lane."

Lane smiled at his audience, the same smile he always smiled at his audience, whether reporting on marauding peace breakers in Bosnia, starving children in Ethiopia, or brawling football players at the university.

"I'm sure Freddie O'Neal has a good explanation, Mark. And we'll have more news, right after this message."

I didn't understand how somebody that shallow could be so likable. And I was too tired to ruminate on it.

The next image on the screen was a man with inky black hair, wearing a blue suit, standing stiffly in front of a gun case.

"Hi, I'm Baxter Cate. And I want to talk to you about responsible gun ownership." He gestured toward the display behind him, his arm moving like animated clay.

I grabbed the remote and started channel-surfing for a movie. I caught a glimpse of Peter O'Toole smiling as somebody whipped him, and I had to give it up. *Lawrence of Arabia* doesn't work on the small screen anyway.

I turned out the light and thought about going to sleep. But that thought sank underneath the others. The one on top was the complex question of who killed Charlie Castro, and why, and why I had to be unlucky enough to find him.

I wished I had called Curtis earlier, but I hadn't.

I hoped Tola Rae hadn't watched the news.

At least I had warned Ramona.

I forced my eyes to close.

Butch had stretched out along my right flank, and Sundance was curled up on the spare pillow, Curtis's pillow when he was there.

Sometimes cats are all that can get you through the night.

Chapter 9

AS SOON AS I reached Curtis's hospital room the next morning, I knew Tola Rae had watched the news, and she hadn't liked it much. Not that she said anything—she excused herself to get a cup of coffee as politely as she had the day before. But her smile was a shade cooler, and something in my gut felt she wasn't glad to see me.

"How're you doing?" I asked Curtis once she was gone.

"Still tired. I'm beginning to wonder if I'll spend the rest of my life tired." His voice was no more than a whisper. Still.

I sat down next to the bed in the chair that Tola Rae had vacated and I took his hand. His skin color wasn't good—it was almost a dull gray—and his eyes weren't their usual sharp blue. I figured he had looked that way yesterday, and I had been so glad to see him I just hadn't noticed.

"You won't. Bullet wounds take time to heal. And a lung is a painful place to be hit because you have to keep breathing. Besides, you're in a hospital. They wake you up at odd hours to give you pills that make you drowsy but don't quite kill the pain. Of course you're going to feel tired in a hospital."

He smiled, sort of. The expression didn't make it past the tube sending oxygen into his nostrils.

"How do you know? When were you in a hospital?"

"Not since I was born, except as a visitor. But I listen to what people tell me."

"Sometimes they kill the pain." He sighed and closed his eyes.

I searched for something to say, and when I couldn't find it, I just sat and held his hand. I hate sitting in hospitals. I was glad Tola Rae was there to stay with him, and I felt a pang of guilt over that.

He opened his eyes. "How are you?"

"I guess you didn't watch the news last night." When he didn't say anything, I had to keep going. "Mike Danken thought I might feel better if I did somebody a favor by shadowing her husband. I found him dead."

"The husband?"

"Yeah." I smiled, but I couldn't hold it. "And there's kind of a vague connection to Jamie Morales. So I'm still in the news."

"So how are you?"

"Oh, hell. I wish none of this were happening. Other than that, I'm fine."

Curtis nodded and squeezed my hand. He closed his eyes again.

We stayed like that awhile, until Tola Rae came back.

I dropped his hand and he opened his eyes.

"I have to go." I glanced from Curtis to Tola Rae and back. "I need to stop by the station and get an update from Matthews."

"You certainly do lead an interesting life," Tola Rae said. "Are you always in the middle of so much excitement?"

The word "excitement" sounded like a synonym for "scandal." I suspected Tola Rae didn't approve of public scandal.

"Fortunately, no. Most of the time it's pretty quiet. I guess my life right now is going something like the way pilots describe their work—hours and hours of boredom punctuated by moments of sheer terror."

Tola Rae didn't find that amusing.

I knew I was looking the worse for the emotional wear of the past four days. I had clapped on my cowboy hat that morning rather than wash my hair because I didn't want to sit around for the hour or so I'd have to spend waiting for it to dry before going out in the cold. And I didn't have the patience for a blow dryer, even if a stream of hot air was good for long hair, which it isn't. I hadn't wanted to deal with the laundry or the dry cleaners, so I was wearing the same brown sweater she had first seen me in. With the same jeans. And no makeup.

She was wearing a winter-white dress in some kind of light wool with a chain of blue pearls that were probably real. Her hair looked as if she might have stopped by a hotel salon on her way to the hospital, and her makeup gave her skin a translucent sheen.

I had to get out of there.

I said good-bye without passing on Ramona's invitation for Christmas dinner. The idea of sitting at the same table with Ramona, Al, and Tola Rae for a meal, much less something as emotionally charged as Christmas dinner, was enough to make me consider changing my name, dying my hair, picking up the Cherokee at the airport, and flying straight to Rio de Janeiro. If I worked out a low flying pattern, I might be able to miss the radar and smuggle the cats past quarantine.

In Rio, it wouldn't be winter.

The glimpse of weather that I had caught on TV the night before said that a storm was coming in—good news for the Squaw Valley ski slopes, if not for the rest of us—but the morning had been clear enough that I had walked to the hospital.

As I came outside I checked the weather out of habit, even though I wasn't really planning to fly.

Thick gray clouds were starting to pile up on the northwest horizon. Flying down to Rio would have to wait. But if I were lucky, the storm would clog the Mount Rose Highway for a couple of days, and Christmas with Ramona and Al would be out.

Take-out chicken with the cats for Christmas wasn't a bad idea. In fact, it was even a good idea. Deke might even want to share, although he always worked a double shift on Christmas, to give people with families the day off.

People who had families they wanted to spend Christmas with, that is.

I took the half block north and two blocks west to the police station at a fast walk. I wanted to get home before the clouds cut off the sun.

I nodded to Danny Sinclair, the officer at the desk, and went straight down the hall.

Seeing Matthews didn't take long. He barely looked up from the mass of papers in front of him. He didn't even offer me coffee.

"This one's going to take awhile," he said. "His wife doesn't know who'd want to kill him, and neither did what's-her-name from the office."

"Letty Rashad," I stuck in.

"Right. And neither of them knows where he was going twice a week. Or the possible significance of the tar and chicken feathers. So we're tracking down everybody who was in or out of Sierra Express yesterday, trying to follow

Castro's movements from house to work. He left the house on time and arrived at work dead. That's all we know right now."

"Well, when you find out what he was involved in, I'd like to know."

"It's fine that you're curious, O'Neal. But you got no reason to keep going on this one, right?"

"Right, Matthews. Merry Christmas."

By the time I was walking out the door, the clouds were almost on top of me. Without the sun, the chill settled down quickly. I forgot about Rio and trotted home.

Light flakes were swirling around me as I reached my front porch. Sundance had been sitting under the winter skeleton of the lilac bush, an orange blob against the varying browns of the branches, the dirt, and the mostly dead lawn. He reached the door in one bound, even before I had turned the key.

Butch was waiting on my desk. He had kicked most of the loose papers to the floor to make himself comfortable.

One good thing about winter. The cats stayed close to home and didn't hunt much. Not many small, warm-blooded animals worth foraging until spring.

I went into the bathroom and closed the window, thus blocking the cat's passageway in and out. I hadn't set up a winter litter box yet, which meant I'd have to let them out again before dark. Neither one liked using a box, but both thought it was better than going out during a storm, and I thought it was better than running up the heating bill by leaving the window open all night long all winter long.

I went back to my desk and picked up the papers Butch had scattered. I was going to have to get back to work soon, back to work seriously, and I knew that.

Making phone calls on a couple of skip-trace jobs seemed like something I could handle.

Nevertheless, my head was down on the desk when the phone rang.

"I just wanted to wish you a merry Christmas," Sandra said.

"Merry Christmas to you, too."

"Between Don's parents and mine, both wanting a piece of their granddaughter, the next few days are shot. But I heard about the mess last night, and I hope you know that I'll make time for you if you want to talk about it."

"Matthews thinks he has that one under control."

"He has a lead?"

"No. But I don't care."

"Oh. How's Curtis?"

"Doing okay, I guess."

"You don't sound sure."

"He doesn't exactly look well, not that I'd expect him to. And his mother is here, so I'm not spending much time with him."

"How are you getting along with her?"

"Okay. I can't help thinking she'd be happier if he were seeing somebody who wore makeup and skirts."

"Are you sure you've given her a chance to like you?"

"No. But I get tired easily, and I don't want to try any harder right now."

"Oh, Freddie. I'm sorry about this, everything that's happened the past three days."

"Thanks. It's not your fault."

"I know." She put her hand over the receiver for a second, and I heard her say something muffled. Then she was back. "Are you going to the lake for Christmas?"

"I don't think so. I know you're going to find this hard to understand, but I think I'd rather be alone."

"Not only do I not understand, I don't think it's a good

idea. With everything that's going on, you need to be around people at Christmas. People who care about you."

I rubbed my eyes with the hand not holding the phone.

"Trust me, Sandra. Being alone is a good idea. What I don't need is the added strain of being around people, whether they care about me or not. I'll be with the cats. I'll be fine."

I waited while she thought about that.

"You could come with us for Christmas. My parents would be glad to see you."

"Your father wouldn't remember me and your mother doesn't know me, and thank you for the offer, but I'd really rather be alone."

"My father would remember you." When I didn't respond, she added, "You're certain?"

"I'm certain." I was too tired to reassure her any longer. "I'll talk with you next week."

While the phone was still in my hand, I called Ramona. I let her think I was going to have Christmas dinner with Curtis in the hospital and told her I'd exchange presents with her before the year was out. It was easier than arguing. I was even too tired to feel guilty about the lie.

I made a trip to the grocery store for cat food, kitty litter, and some microwavable cartons that claimed to contain dinners, rented half a dozen videos, came home, took a shower, and settled down in my bedroom for a long, quiet weekend.

All in all, it felt pretty good. I was right. I needed the peace and quiet.

I walked to the hospital to see Curtis each of the next three mornings. The storm wasn't a bad one, and the neighborhood looked better after the light snowfall covered up the brown lawns. I focused on the medical center floor from the front door to the elevator to avoid the Christmas decorations, and Curtis was too tired to ask what I was doing for Christmas. Tola Rae took her coffee breaks, and I sat quietly by the bed until she got back. She tried small talk once, but I didn't help her out.

Christmas Eve I joined Deke for dinner in the Mother Lode coffee shop. He didn't seem surprised that I'd decided to opt out of social obligations for the next day.

"Don't hide for too long, though," he warned. "It could get to be a habit. And then you don't want to be around people at all no more."

I would have argued with him, would have said I wasn't hiding, but I suspected he was right.

By the day after Christmas—either despite or because of his warning—I was ready to rejoin the living.

I sat down at my desk and started making the phone calls on the two skip-trace jobs that I had neglected the week before, the man who had bailed on child support and the woman who had ignored a court judgment on a contract dispute. There must have been something to say for the after-Christmas spirit, because I hit three people in a row who wanted to talk.

The doorbell rang while I was still listening. I carried the phone with me to answer it.

Louise Danken, bundled up in a green parka over black pants and boots, smiled uncertainly from the porch. I motioned her in and pointed toward one of the black-and-white cowhide chairs in front of my desk. When I could, I hung up.

"I'm sorry to barge in," she said. "I tried to call."

"The line's been busy. I'm sorry. I probably ought to get call waiting."

"I wanted to ask you over for tea this afternoon."

"Thanks for the invitation, but I took a couple of days off, and I'm trying to catch up. Could we make it another day?"

She shook her head. "Please. You need to talk to Mike."

"Thanks. Really. But I'm doing fine."

"No, not for you. For Mike. He's taking this all personally. He decided to investigate Charlie Castro's murder on his own."

"Oh, God. Why?"

"God. Exactly. He thinks God wants him to do it."

"Shit."

The word came out unbidden. Her eyes widened, and I was sorry I said it.

"Roy Matthews could do a better job telling him to stay out of it than I could," I added.

"I've asked him, too. And Elena Castro. I need all the help I can get. Please."

I almost swore again. "What time?"

"Four o'clock."

"Okay. See you then."

Louise Danken smiled her perfect Annette Funicello smile then stood and held out her hand. I stood and took it. I was only about eight inches taller.

I got back on the phone after she left and worked until quarter to four with a short lunch break. I had solid leads on the whereabouts of both people I was looking for, leads I could follow up that evening or the next day.

I went to the closet for my denim jacket, remembering after I got there that it was gone. Deke might have taken it to the cleaners, or he might have burned it. I'd have to ask him. I hoped he hadn't burned my navy sweater.

The indirect rays of the afternoon sun weren't going to be warm enough, especially on the way back. I left with my sheepskin jacket over my arm.

I arrived at the combination house and church a little after four. One of the cars parked in front belonged to Matthews.

The other was a white Ford Escort with a battered passenger side door.

Since it was office hours, I walked right in, as the sign told me to do. The converted living room was still decorated for Christmas. I had been avoiding reminders of Christmas whenever possible, but the overload of tinsel and green was a little much to ignore.

Matthews was standing in the corner next to the fireplace-turned-altar, heavy coat covering the folding chair next to him. His face was lowered toward a teacup and saucer too fragile for his beefy hands, causing his jowls to spread over his shirt collar.

"Danken not here yet?" I asked.

He shook his head. "And I can't stay. The Castro woman is in the kitchen with Louise. She doesn't want to stay, either."

"That makes three of us."

"Have some tea." He handed me the cup and saucer and picked up his coat. "Don't worry about germs. I didn't take a sip. I don't like tea."

"What's going on?"

"I probably know just what you do. Louise says Mike is investigating on his own. She doesn't want him to. Neither do I. But I got a deskload of paperwork to get back to, including stuff the DA wants on the Morales kid."

"Jamie Morales?" I thought that was finished.

"Robert. They're gonna make some kind of plea bargain, maybe even probation."

"That's probably a good idea." I looked for a place to set the cup and saucer. I wouldn't have minded some tea, but I wanted it warm.

"You sure you don't object?"

"You kidding? I don't want to testify against the boy in

court. And Curtis won't be well enough for weeks. And with luck, he'll be scared straight."

He nodded. Matthews always had bags under his eyes, pulling the lower lids down until you could see a touch of red. I had never seen the circles quite so dark, as if he couldn't get enough sleep for the rest of his life.

"What about the Castro murder?" I asked.

"No leads. And don't get any ideas. I don't want Mike in it and I don't want you in it."

"Hey." I held my hands up in a gesture of surrender.

"I have no reason to be involved."

He nodded again.

"I gotta say good-bye to Louise." He had started toward the archway before he finished speaking.

I moved a dry pine branch enough to set the saucer on the altar, then felt guilty and took it back. I followed Matthews, figuring the kitchen was the place to go.

We almost collided in the hall as he headed back toward the front door. He must have said good-bye to Louise in record time.

"Later," he said, without stopping.

The kitchen was large enough to accommodate a serious cook. The wide window over the sink would have caught the early morning light, something to look forward to if you were fixing breakfast. On this winter afternoon, overhead fluorescent lights had been turned on.

Louise Danken and Elena Castro were seated in a breakfast nook, a three-sided projection into the backyard that was a popular feature in early fifties tract homes. Pale peach café curtains had been pulled back on their double rod, exposing a view of a stark deciduous tree. I can never recognize trees without their leaves.

"Oh, Freddie, I'm sorry," Louise said, sliding out from

behind the table. "I should have been out there to greet you."

"Don't worry." I put the cup and saucer on the sink.

"Do you want tea?" she asked.

"Sure."

Elena Castro glared at me through puffy eyes. She hadn't been crying recently, but she had been crying long.

"I got to go now," she said. "I have two children who will need dinner. And I am so lucky to have two children at home."

"You are," I answered, as politely as I could.

"I lost my husband, so I am a widow now. You know what they call a mother who loses her children?"

She seemed to be waiting for an answer, so I said, "No, I don't."

"Nothing. That's what they call her. My cousin Elva is nothing. Losing your children is so terrible there is no word for it."

"I'm sorry. But it wasn't my fault. And she still has Robert."

"Please," Louise said. "Please. I don't know what to say to either of you. You have both suffered so terribly over this. Please. Please. Sit down, have some tea, and wait for Mike to get here."

"I am sorry I cannot wait, Louise." Elena slid out from her side of the table. "Tell Mike it's okay. I don't hold him responsible for anything."

Louise had turned on the gas flame under the tea kettle.

"Just a minute, Freddie," she said apologetically.

She followed Elena into the hall and returned almost immediately. The kettle wasn't quite whistling. She put a fresh tea bag in a clean cup and leaned against the sink.

"I really wanted this to work," she said.

"It isn't your fault. Do you know where Mike is?"

"No."

I really wanted to leave. More than anything, I wanted to leave. But I accepted a cup of tea and I sat down to wait with her.

We were sitting on the wrong side of the house to see the sunset. We knew when it happened because the backyard turned from indigo to black.

Louise tried to chat for a while, but she didn't have Tola Rae's talent for small talk, and God knows I don't either. Although we never talked about God.

I left about seven because I was getting hungry and I figured I could catch Deke at the Mother Lode. I hoped she would fix herself something to eat.

And I hoped, for her sake, that Mike Danken came home soon.

Chapter
10

MIKE DANKEN CALLED me the next morning.

"I'm sorry I missed you last night," he said. "But something came up in the Castro murder case, and I needed to stay with it."

"Have you told Matthews about it?" I asked.

The good thing about the delay was that I'd had time to think about what I ought to say to him. I wake up before dawn every once in a while, sometimes in a cold sweat, sometimes in a fit of awful clarity, although the clarity too often fades before the sunrise. Some mornings, like that one, the insomnia lasts just long enough to think through the situation.

"No. He's overworked as it is, Freddie, you know that. I thought I'd just quietly help him out."

"Not a good idea, Mike. You're not a cop anymore. You don't have official status, you don't have a partner, you don't have backup. You don't have a gun."

"I know what to do, though, and I'll turn it all over to Roy when I have something solid. I promise I won't do anything dangerous. How's that?"

Hard for me to argue with, because I'd said the same thing too often myself. This wasn't following my predawn scenario.

"If you need help and you can't get Matthews, will you call me?"

"I don't think it will come to that. But I'll remember the offer."

After I'd hung up, I felt vaguely guilty. I hadn't done what Louise had asked or what Matthews had wanted. I hadn't argued as forcefully with him as I had with myself at four-thirty that morning. But Mike Danken was an adult, and he had the right to make his own decisions.

I set the guilt aside and left the house, first to see Curtis, then to follow the skip-trace leads I had generated the day before for the two clients I had been putting off. Charlie Castro was not my problem, and neither was Mike Danken.

When I got to Curtis's room, I was surprised to find him on his feet. He still had the pronged tube sending oxygen to his nostrils, but he was otherwise free of machines. He was standing by the window, dressed in his own light-blue flannel bathrobe and slippers, with his hand on Tola Rae's shoulder.

"Wow," I said. "You're better."

"I think so." The voice was still a whisper.

He smiled, though. I was so happy to see him standing and smiling that I would have walked over and kissed him if Tola Rae hadn't been there.

I hadn't realized, not even at 4:30 A.M., how much I missed being around him. Talking to him. Arguing with him. Hanging out and watching television, eating Chinese take-out.

"If you'll excuse me," Tola Rae said, "I'm ready for a fresh cup of coffee."

She patted Curtis's hand, the one that was on her shoulder,

and helped him back to the bed. He sat down on the edge and swung his legs up, but he didn't lie back on the raised pillows.

"Have I been chasing you out?" I asked.

"Oh, no, nothing like that. You've been acting a little shy, though, like a cat that wasn't raised around people, and I thought I'd give you time to get used to me before I try to feed you again."

Curtis made a sound that would have been a chuckle before the bullet wound, then winced. I tried to find a smile in Tola Rae's face. She looked as wintry as a northern cloud formation to me, but maybe I just wasn't used to her yet.

"Ramona—my mother—wants to meet you while you're in Reno." I wasn't certain the sentence was going to come out whole until it was in the air.

Tola Rae nodded. "She said that, over the phone. I let her know I was going to be here for a while. No hurry."

"Oh, hell. She told you she had wanted you to come for Christmas."

"And she hoped we all had a good time together."

"I'm sorry. I needed to be alone."

"That's what Curtis said you'd say."

"Did he tell you I wasn't going to be able to deal with exchanging presents right now?"

"Yes. He suggested—and I agreed—that we might substitute a small celebration once he's out of the hospital." She stood with her arms crossed and her head slightly lowered, regarding me as if she were assessing my worth. "I understand you're a student of history, that you know a lot about Nevada and the Old West."

"Not really. Mostly I watch old movies."

She raised her eyebrows and I stopped.

"You've told Curtis stories about Indians who lived in a place called the Lost City, an archaeological treasure that was flooded when Hoover Dam created Lake Mead, because nobody cared to protect it. About the cave paintings, and the bone fragments that may have been gaming dice, twenty thousand years before Las Vegas. That information isn't from some John Ford epic. Curtis thinks you may be one of those Indians reincarnated."

"He said all that with a tube up his nose?"

I didn't quite get a laugh out of her, but she tried.

"No, he'd told me about the Indians before. And that you gamble, and that sometimes you need to go into your cave."

"I don't paint, though."

"You've never tried," Curtis whispered. "You like art. And you have a good eye, when you remember to use it."

I ignored that. "And I'm really not a student of history. Haven't been for years."

"Not true," Curtis whispered.

"You can come in, if you like," Tola Rae said.

I realized I was still standing in the doorway.

"And I don't believe in reincarnation." I took a couple of tentative steps toward the bed.

"I'll go get my coffee now," Tola Rae said. "I actually do want a fresh cup. While I'm gone, you can think about whether you want to have dinner with me tonight."

I waited until she was out the door before I sat down on the bed and took Curtis's hand.

"I thought I'd blown it with her when I found the body in the parking lot," I said.

"She wasn't happy about it," he whispered, "but she's keeping an open mind. Believe it or not, she's good at keeping an open mind."

"Maybe better than I am. Do you really think I'm a reincarnated cave-dwelling Indian?"

"I think it's possible. I think a lot of things are possible."

"You lived in Southern California too long."

He squeezed my hand. "Tell me what's going on."

"Mike Danken is investigating the Castro murder on his own. His wife wanted me to talk him out of it, but I couldn't after he said the magic words—he'd call for help if he thinks he's in danger."

"Do you believe him?"

"I want to. Would a minister lie?"

"Not intentionally. What about Morales?"

"Jamie Morales is still dead. They're working out a plea bargain for Robert."

"Good. About Robert."

"That's what I thought. And I didn't think you'd want to testify against him."

"No, not really. When are you going to stop beating yourself up about Jamie?"

"Maybe not till he's alive again. Think you can convince me to believe in reincarnation?"

Curtis wheezed and winced. "Not in this lifetime. And you have to forgive yourself for shooting Jamie Morales anyway."

"I've forgiven myself for shooting him. Just not for killing him. I know it's a fine distinction. But it's a real one."

"Have you given up the idea of talking to his mother?"

"For now, at least. Her cousin reduced me to silence. God only knows what *she* could do."

He leaned back against the raised pillows and closed his eyes.

"Are you tired?"

He nodded. "But I'm glad you're here. I'm glad we're both here."

"Me too."

"Have you decided about dinner?" Tola Rae was in the doorway, white foam cup in hand.

"Sure. I'll be happy to have dinner with you."

"Fine. Seven o'clock. You can pick me up."

"Okay. And I've meant to ask you—did you happen to pick up some packages from the security guard at the mall?"

"Yes, I did. And I've been holding two boxes, one containing a leopard-print vest and one containing a man's navy blue sweater, size extra large, until someone asked about them."

"Thanks. Maybe I could get them tonight."

"Fine."

The good-byes were a little awkward. Shaking hands didn't seem right, and I couldn't bring myself to hug her. I just sort of eased past her to the door.

I was one-for-two on the cases that afternoon. I located the woman who defaulted on the court judgment, but I couldn't find the deadbeat dad. The leads on that one dried up.

Dinner with Tola Rae was easier than I had expected. She asked for more stories about the cave dwellers of Pueblo del Valle, later renamed the Lost City, than I could tell, although I did explain that it may not be quite accurate to call them Indians. They may have been ancestors of the Paiutes, but that isn't exactly the same thing. I'm not a historian, and I explained that. Nevertheless, I have a sense of what good history is.

She had been waiting for me at the door to the apartment building with packages in hand when I arrived to pick her up, and she insisted that I drop her off in front. Either Curtis had told her I might not want to go in, or she had figured it out for herself. Either way, I was grateful.

The next day I took a quick trip to Lake Tahoe to see Ramona and Al. Actually, it was a slow trip, because the highway was still slick from the last storm. Snow tires or chains required. I was glad I was the one driving, not

Ramona. She could have done it, but it would have made us both nervous.

Ramona had to show me her Christmas outfit, a suede jacket and pants dripping bright red fringe. And she liked the leopard-print vest. Curtis had been right about that. Al said polite things about the sweater.

They gave me a gift certificate from a Western wear store. A real one, not a chain.

"You need new boots," Ramona said. "And I can't pick them out for you."

"You're looking great, Al," I told him, after I had thanked them, honestly, for the gift. I did need new boots. And the certificate was enough to cover a good pair of boots and a new denim jacket as well.

"I'm feeling great, too. I still get tired easily, but the doctor tells me I'll get my old energy back."

Al didn't really look great. He looked like an old man who would never get his energy back. Ramona, with her warm copper curls and surgically firmed chin, could have passed in a soft light for half his age. Or about my age.

I wondered if Curtis would still be tired three months down the line. I hoped not. I hoped the recovery curve for bullet wounds was sharper than the one for heart attacks.

"Do you know yet when Curtis will be out of the hospital?" Ramona asked.

"No. Soon, though. He's a lot better."

"If Tola Rae doesn't want to leave him, I could drive down to Reno. The three of us could have lunch at that little French place on South Virginia. I've enjoyed talking to her on the phone, and I'm looking forward to meeting her."

"And she's looking forward to meeting you."

Unfortunately that was true. Tola Rae did want to meet Ramona. I was the only one uncomfortable with the idea. I considered suggesting that they meet without me, but that might be worse. I'd have to think about it.

"She seems like such a nice person. I told her how glad I was she was in Reno at such a difficult time. You spent too much time alone before you met Curtis, and I didn't want you going back to that again. I'm sure her presence has been a comfort to both of you."

"You're right, Ramona, it has."

"You seem to be doing so well. I'm glad you were able to handle killing that boy."

I managed to get out of there right after dinner with my blood pressure only slightly elevated.

The familiar drive down the Mount Rose Highway had its usual calming effect on me, even though I had to concentrate because of the ice. When I rounded a corner and suddenly found myself out of the trees, with the blazing neon lights of the city spread out below, dwindling into the darkness of the desert beyond, I was more relaxed than I had been in days.

The feeling lasted until I was home and checking the messages on my answering machine.

One was from Baxter Cate.

"I haven't given up," he said.

I didn't care. To hell with him. I wouldn't be his shill.

The second was from Louise Danken.

"Mike hasn't come home. Can you call me when you get in? Please. No matter what time it is."

It was a little before eleven. According to the machine, she had called about a half hour earlier. I pushed the buttons for her number. I could tell from the way she cried "Hello?" that she hoped it was Mike.

"How long has he been gone?" I asked.

"He left late this afternoon. I know it had to do with

Charlie Castro, but he wouldn't tell me where he was going."

"He may show up yet with a good explanation. If you don't hear from him by morning, call Matthews. He may be able to get the missing persons guys to move on it. Or even do something himself."

"I thought you might be able to do something." There was an edge to her voice that I couldn't quite decipher.

"I have no idea where to start looking for him. So there's nothing I could do tonight. How's this—I'll call you first thing in the morning, and if you need to go to the police station, I'll go with you."

"That sounds sensible. I've been worried, and I may be overreacting."

I was more worried that she wasn't overreacting.

"Fix some cocoa, watch a movie," I said.

"Take two aspirin?"

"Good idea."

"And I will call you in the morning."

I turned on the television and clicked my way through the stations a couple of times, waiting for the news. When Lane Josten finally started reading from the TelePrompTer, he had no items about anyone named Danken or Morales or Castro or Breckinridge or O'Neal.

I was so relieved that I curled up between the cats and slept through the night.

Chapter
11

THE PHONE WOKE me up. Louise Danken wanted to know how quickly I could meet her at the police station.

I asked her to give me half an hour.

She was waiting on the front steps, wearing her green parka and black pants and boots. Her dark hair had been pulled back and clipped, but a stray lock betrayed its unwashed state. Her face was the color of concrete, her eyes bloodshot from too many tears and too little sleep.

"Thank you for coming," she said.

"Well, I told Mike I'd back him up if he got into trouble."

"I know."

That had been the edge in her voice the night before. He had told her I'd be his backup. I was pissed that he had told her that but hadn't told one of us where he was going. And I was afraid he hadn't kept his promise about staying out of danger.

Not as afraid as Louise was. And not as pissed as Matthews was when we sat down at his desk—or Louise sat, since there was only one chair—and he heard that Mike hadn't come home the night before.

He slapped a form in front of Louise.

"Fill it out. And then let me handle it. Both of you." He glared at each of us in turn.

I stared out the window at the gray light.

Louise began to cry. I only knew because I turned to look when I heard the pen hit the desk and bounce. She didn't sob or anything. And her eyes didn't leave Matthews's face until he blinked, unable to watch the flood.

"What'd he tell you?" Matthews asked.

"That he wouldn't do anything dangerous. That he would call Freddie if he needed backup, call you when he had something solid."

Matthews had an excuse to glare at me, and he took it.

"I tried. I really did," I said.

"Okay. Do you know where he started?" he asked Louise.

"Just the Castro family and the young woman at Sierra Express. He didn't have anything that you didn't. Except more time, he said. And the hope that someone might talk to him who wouldn't talk to the police." She had fished a tissue from her pocket and blotted her eyes without missing a beat.

"We'll do what we can. Go home and stay there. And you." Matthews glared at me again. "I can't tell you to stay home. I know you need to visit the hospital. But I can tell you that you don't have a client here, and this is an open police investigation with which I do not want you interfering. Is that understood?" He punched each word, like Winston Churchill making a speech.

"Yes, sir." I fought the impulse to salute.

"I need to fill out the form," Louise said. "I want this to be official."

Matthews and I watched in silence as she picked up the pen, holding it with care, and neatly printed the required information, never going outside the lines. When there was a box to check, she did so with clean diagonals, corner to corner. Then she handed Matthews the pen.

"Thank you for your help," she said.

She got up and headed for the door without waiting to see if I followed.

I shrugged a quick good-bye to Matthews.

"I mean it," he called after me. "I got one dead body and one missing friend already. Don't mess with this."

Danny Sinclair, the redheaded desk sergeant, was on the phone. I ignored him and caught up with Louise again on the front steps, where she had stopped to blot her eyes.

"I can go to Sierra Express and talk to Letty Rashad on my own," I said. "But I'll need your help with Elena Castro. If I try to talk to her, she'll throw a chair at me."

"Detective Matthews told you not to do this," Louise whispered.

"I know. But he'd probably be disappointed if I paid attention. He heard you say Mike expected me to back him up. He knows I have to."

"Do you?"

"Yes."

"You don't sound as if you want to."

I started to say, "Shit, no," and caught myself in time. Louise Danken looked sad enough without that.

"Okay. In an ideal world, I'd leave it to Matthews. He's a good guy, and I trust him. But Mike was right, Matthews is overworked. And I'm not certain Mike would have gotten involved in this at all if he hadn't wanted to help me."

"He would—" Louise started, but I held up my hand and cut her off.

"Maybe. But he wanted to help me, and I owe him. And I promised. And I don't ever want to look in the bathroom mirror and see a woman who broke a promise to back up a friend staring at me, not unless I'm too crippled to move.

And this speech is starting to get embarrassing. So will you call Elena Castro and ask her to talk to me?"

"All right. Yes."

I patted her on the shoulder and walked away. I had left the Jeep at home. The next decision was whether to detour to Washoe Medical to see Curtis before I picked it up or after, on my way to Sierra Express.

Better yet, I could stop by the hospital after I had talked to Letty Rashad, when I had something positive to say. If I had something positive to say.

Louise was right. I didn't want to do this. I felt as if I had just taken a seat at a poker table and been handed someone else's cards with the admonition to play, not fold. How the hell did I know what was going on in the game?

I crossed Second Street and walked south on High, with my internal grumbling slowly fading. The sun was bright, and the day was turning into one of those late December freaks, where the weather report is calling for temperatures in the forties, but your body argues that it has to be spring. In some cities people talk about windchill factors. Other cities, and Reno is one of them, have a clear sky factor, or something like that. You start looking for crocuses in the warm sun, think you've rediscovered hope, but patches of snow are still lurking in the shade, and the tree roots know better than to stir.

I got in the Jeep and drove to Sierra Express.

The parking lot was almost empty. The after-Christmas slump. Four white panel trucks with the blue stylized mountain logos sat nosed against the side fence, already coated with the dust of disuse. Half a dozen cars, including Letty Rashad's red Toyota, were parked in front of the squat building. I left the Jeep in the same corner it had occupied the week before and walked across the asphalt to the office door.

Letty Rashad was sitting behind a steel desk with a disorder of papers worse than my own spread out on it. She was talking on the telephone, and almost dropped the receiver when she recognized me.

I sat down in one of three white plastic chairs that seemed to have been placed in arbitrary slots against the wall and glanced around the room as Letty checked something on her computer terminal and fumbled her way out of the conversation. One round table with old magazines. Two tall steel filing cabinets. A scattering of framed licenses. One door leading into the building, one leading out. Nothing personal. Nothing to show that a human being had claimed this space as her own. Not even a Christmas card, although that wasn't necessarily bad.

The receiver clattered into place.

"What do you want?" she asked.

"How long have you worked here?" I countered.

"What? What do you mean?" Her hands reached out for the papers, long fingers operating separately, trying to organize the odd white sheets into stacks, even as her wide, dark eyes locked onto mine.

"Just that." I held out my hands. "No gun. No threat. Just a question. How long have you worked here?"

"Six months."

"And Charlie Castro?"

"I told all this to the officer, the woman. I told her everything I know." The eyes jerked, but she stayed with me.

"Did you tell it again to Mike Danken?"

"Why do you want to know?"

"Because his wife says he didn't come home last night, and I promised to help her out."

"Aren't you wonderful, always helping people out."

A surge of adrenaline almost short-circuited my thought processes, but I waited until it subsided.

"I guess you wouldn't think so," I answered. "Would you rather talk about Jamie Morales?"

"I'd rather not talk to you at all."

"And you don't have to. We can sit here in silence."

The phone rang. Letty hesitated for a moment, then pushed her hair behind her ear and answered it. By the time she found the computer file the caller wanted, her wavy black mane had popped loose and enveloped the receiver. She hung up and stared at me.

I made a show of getting comfortable in the stiff, plastic chair.

"Jamie wanted the earrings for his mother. He didn't have money to buy her a Christmas present. He saw your friend buy the earrings, and he wanted them for his mother."

I wanted to tell her that he should have bought a present for his mother instead of a gun for himself, but it wouldn't have helped. "His brother told you that?"

She nodded. "Robert tried to talk him out of it. Jamie wouldn't listen. Jamie wouldn't listen to nobody, and you shouldn't blame his mother for what he did."

"You're probably right."

"And what he did was wrong, okay. But you shouldn't have killed him, either."

A week ago, that judgment would have done bad things to my head. Time was helping.

"What would you have done?" I asked. Calmly. I asked it calmly.

Letty evidently hadn't considered that.

"I don't know," she said, pushing her hair back. "Talked to him, maybe."

"Even after he shot your friend? My friend was lying on the ground bleeding, and Jamie still had his gun." And maybe he wasn't turning away. Time was making the moment hazier, not clearer.

"Couldn't you have fired in the air?"

"Maybe I could have. But then he might have shot me."

She frowned, uncertain. "You were scared? That's why you shot him? You were scared?"

"I was terrified." I took a deep breath and kept going. "I didn't know Jamie. I knew Curtis. And Curtis was bleeding, maybe dying, and I was scared shitless I'd be next. And so I shot."

"Yeah, okay." She looked down at the desk and started gathering papers together, apparently into random stacks. "I would have been scared, too. Robert was scared. That's why he ran away."

"How do you know the family?"

"My parents live next door to Charlie and Elena Castro, so I grew up knowing them. Charlie got me this job. Elena had the boys over all the time. They were sort of like her nephews or something. Mrs. Morales was working nights, she had to work two jobs all the time, so Elena watched the boys along with her own."

"What about Mr. Morales?"

Letty shrugged. "Nobody ever talked about him. I guess there was one—Jamie and Robert had to have a father—but nobody ever talked about him."

"Okay. You said you started working here six months ago. That would have been June. Where were you going to school?"

"Truckee Meadows. I got my A.A. in Business. Why do you want to know all this?"

"I want to know where Mike Danken is. Mike was trying to find out what happened to Charlie Castro. And you're my best connection to Charlie Castro."

"I don't know nothing about his murder."

I held up my hand. "I believe you. At the same time, I think you may have information that could help me. And maybe neither one of us will know what that information is unless we talk. You work here, where Charlie Castro worked and where his body was found. Here is where I have to start."

Letty hesitated, and I waited. Too long. I heard a car door slam outside, and then a second slam shortly after.

"My boss is here," she said. "You're going to have to leave."

"When can I get in touch with you?"

"I don't know."

The door from the parking lot swung open, and the small office was suddenly filled with the presence of two men, one in plaid shirt and down vest and the other in a worn, brown leather bomber jacket.

"Can I help you?" the man in the vest asked. He didn't look as if he wanted to help anyone. The top of his face was narrow, as if the doctor had grabbed the wrong spot with the forceps when he was born, pinching his eyes into his nose. His jaw flared below, already blue, a five o'clock shadow before noon. His lips were thin and tight, matching his eyes.

I stood up and introduced myself. Neither man was taller than I am, but they both had me on girth, their beer bellies resting on ornate metal belt buckles. The buckles matched. I didn't recognize the insignia, a gold circle within a silver star.

The man in the bomber jacket had the kind of face you see in the background of organized crime reunion photos— nose pushed toward the left, right eye sinking into the cheekbone. I found myself wishing I were closer to the door.

"She found Charlie Castro's body," Letty volunteered.

The man in the vest frowned.

"I didn't catch your name," I said.

"Kovanda. Joe Kovanda." He didn't hold out his hand. "We told everything to the police. And I have work for Letty to do. She doesn't have time to talk to you."

"Sorry to have taken her away from her job. It wasn't her fault."

"Okay." Kovanda gestured, and the man in the bomber jacket moved away from the door. "Don't do it again."

"Mind if I leave a card?"

Kovanda shrugged, and I took that as a positive sign. I carefully placed a business card on Letty's desk. Her hands were still splayed across the papers.

"Thanks for your time," I said. That wasn't quite what I wanted to say, but she looked frightened, and I didn't want to make things worse for her. I nodded at the two men and left.

The morning seemed just a little chillier when I stepped outside. I looked for a cloud and found a mass of them in the northwest, moving down the line of the Sierras toward the city. New storm coming in.

I didn't have anything good to say, but I decided I couldn't put off Washoe Medical any longer. Deke had said I shouldn't treat Curtis as if he were weak. Still, I was having trouble treating him as if he were strong.

My stomach was growling as I drove the Jeep up the circular ramp into the Washoe Medical parking lot. It was probably getting close to lunchtime, and I hadn't even had a cup of coffee. A spot above my left eye was beginning to ache, a sure sign of caffeine withdrawal. The lot was crowded, but I found a narrow space in the corner.

The old man in the information booth said "Good morning" as I walked past. I returned the greeting. I was starting to feel like a regular. I crossed the pavement to the front door of the hospital.

The Christmas tree was still up.

I kept my head down until I reached the elevators. This, too, shall pass. I could keep my head down for the three days until the new year, and then the decorations would disappear. The cards would go into the fireplaces, the dead firs would follow, all the senior citizens would complain about smoke pollution affecting their lungs, and the holidays would be over for another year. I could handle it.

I knew something was wrong when I entered the room. Tola Rae was sitting in the chair next to the window, one hand covering her eyes.

Curtis was lying flat with an oxygen mask covering his nose and mouth. He was reconnected to the machine that kept track of his heartbeat, and his skin was gray again.

Tola Rae looked up when she heard my step. She put a finger to her lips, then pointed to the hall. I backed through the doorway, and she followed.

"Pneumonia," she whispered.

"What? How? He was doing so well." I stumbled all over the words.

"He was pushing too hard, trying to get back on his feet. You can come in and sit for a while if you want, but I don't think he'll be able to talk." Her face was almost as gray as Curtis's. The lines around her eyes had deepened, aging her ten years from the woman I had picked up at the airport ten days earlier.

"How serious is it?"

"The doctor says he's responding to the antibiotics. I can't see it. And under the circumstances, any infection is serious."

"Oh, God."

Tola Rae reached out and took my hand. Her fingers were thin and cold.

"Serious isn't hopeless," she said. "Curtis won't give up. And he wouldn't want you to, either."

"I know."

"I've left a message for that nice minister, Danken, but he hasn't called. If you see him, let him know that I believe in penicillin, but prayer doesn't hurt."

Ordinarily, I would have forced a smile. It was all I could do to force the words.

"He's missing."

"Oh, dear." She only faltered for a second. "What happened?"

"He wanted to look into the Charlie Castro murder—the body in the car trunk—himself. He didn't come home last night."

"Does anyone have any idea where he is?"

"No. His wife has asked me to see what I can find out."

"And you were coming to tell Curtis about it. He has appreciated—we have both appreciated—the way you talk to him, as if everything is normal. Will you be all right?"

"I suppose. I think so. Is there anything I can do for you?"

"Not right now." She squeezed my fingers. "Although you might explain to your mother that I'm really not putting her off. I would love to have lunch with her soon."

"I'll tell her." I returned the squeeze as best I could. "If Curtis wakes up, let him know I was here."

We parted awkwardly, not ready to hug each other. Or if she was ready, I wasn't.

I retraced my steps to the parking lot, head lower than when I came, slipping quietly past the man in the information booth.

I had planned to stop by the small church to check with Louise Danken. A phone call would have to do.

My stomach growled again as I drove down the ramp, and the spot above my right eye was reminding me that I still hadn't had coffee. I swung down Wells Avenue and picked up a hamburger and fries and a large cup of hot black liquid at a drive-through fast-food stand. I was so anxious to get to the coffee that I slopped some on my jeans.

For a moment I had a vision of third-degree burns and a million-dollar lawsuit, but a napkin sopped up the excess, and my thigh cooled quickly in the breeze from the open window. Still, I put the lid back on the cup and kept it there until I got home.

I played messages while I devoured the lunch, such as it was. When Butch and Sundance suddenly appeared, Butch on the desk and Sundance at my feet, I remembered that I hadn't fed them before I left. I pulled out part of the burger and split it between them.

No word from anyone about Mike Danken. I didn't much care about other clients right then.

Louise Danken answered the phone almost before it rang. She gave me Elena Castro's address and phone number, although she couldn't guarantee cooperation. Elena wasn't happy about my involvement.

I tried to get Sandra next, but she was away from her desk. If there was something going on at Sierra Express, and if it was in the *Herald*'s files, Sandra could find it quicker than I could.

And then I called Ramona.

"Is Curtis all right?" she asked. "Tola Rae sounded so subdued when I called this morning. She said something about pneumonia."

"Curtis is in serious condition, and Tola Rae is pretty strung out. I know she appreciates your concern, and she said to let you know that she isn't putting you off, but maybe you could give it—give her—a rest for a day or two."

"Curtis is going to come through this just fine," Ramona said firmly. "I believe that. And Tola Rae needs to get out of the hospital room. Spending too much time in a hospital room saps your strength. She needs to get out among the healthy a little more."

I thought about Ramona, and the time she had spent sitting in a hospital room with Al. Ramona needed to get out among the healthy a little more.

"You may be right, but she wants to sit with Curtis."

"I may come down and surprise her—take her out to that little French place on South Virginia. I can't remember the name, it used to be something else."

"Every place used to be something else." I didn't have the strength to argue. And maybe Tola Rae should get out. Maybe she and Ramona could forge some kind of bond out of this.

"I don't know. It's odd, what stays the same. Like Woolworth's."

"What?"

"Woolworth's is still there. The old ten-cent store is still on Virginia, when so many other things have changed. Gray Reid Wright's was such a fine department store, and now it's an outlet mall, but Woolworth's is still there. Did I tell you about the time I saw Tony Curtis and Piper Laurie in front of Woolworth's?"

"No."

"They were in Reno filming *Johnny Dark*. It must have been more than forty years ago. You ought to watch it sometime, if you want to see what Reno was like then. That movie and *5 Against the House*, with Guy Madison and Kim Novak."

I struggled with my rising anger. There had to be a reason why my mother had chosen this moment to talk about old movies.

"How's Al?"

"Oh, he's fine. I'm hoping that when the weather is warmer, I can get him to start taking walks. He spends all his time watching television, and it isn't good for him. He should exercise."

"You're right, Ramona. Al should get out of the house. Tell you what. There's a storm moving in, and I don't think you should try to drive down here. But tomorrow or the next day, depending on the weather, I'll drive up, and you and Al and I can have lunch at the Cal-Neva. If Al doesn't want to go, I'll take you."

"What about Tola Rae?"

"We'll do that, too. When she's ready. Okay?"

"I'd be happy to drive down there, you know."

"I know. But I don't want you driving on icy roads."

I couldn't believe I'd said that. It was true, though. I would have worried about her driving down the Mount Rose Highway, even with chains on her car, when a storm was moving in.

She had to take a minute to digest what I'd said.

"I'm not old," she finally answered. "I can drive."

I could hear the pain in her voice.

"I'm sorry. Do what you want to do."

"I'll talk to you tomorrow. Neither one of us should drive through the mountains if a storm is coming in."

"Good idea. Talk to you then."

I hung up the phone and shut my eyes. There had to be an easier way to live, if I could only figure it out.

A claw in my knee reminded me that I still hadn't fed the cats. The piece of hamburger had been just an appetizer. And even though it felt like spring, it was still winter, still a bad time for foraging. Bad for them, good for me. No remnants of small rodents on the kitchen floor.

I split a can of something that smelled far worse than the hamburger into two bowls. The cats thought it was great.

I picked up the scrap of paper with Elena Castro's address and left the house again. The Castros lived in Sparks, in one of the tract homes off York Way that had looked pretty good a couple of decades earlier.

Elena answered the door when I knocked.

"I don't want to talk to you," she said.

"Oh, hell. I don't want to talk to you, either. But Mike

Danken has been missing for close to twenty-four hours now, and if he doesn't turn up soon, we gotta figure we're looking for a corpse. So, do you talk or not?"

She hesitated. A voice behind her said, "It's all right. I'll leave."

Elena stepped aside and motioned me in.

The living room was small, barely room enough for a sofa, two chairs, and a large television set tuned to one of the daytime talk shows. A woman who looked very much like an older version of Elena rose from the sofa.

"This is my cousin," Elena said. "Elva Morales."

Chapter
12

THE SEMANTIC DISTINCTIONS among the responsibility words—blame, fault, guilt—have to do with the difference between a simple practical shortcoming and moral culpability. And it's easy to get that right in your head. I had come to terms with the fact that I could be blamed for Jamie Morales's death because I had pulled a gun and shot him, even though I believed I was shooting in self-defense and hadn't intended to kill. That was simple enough—a practical shortcoming at worst. He was dead because I shot and I didn't miss. And I thought I was certain, just as certain as Deke and Matthews and Tola Rae and Curtis were, that I had no moral culpability and, therefore, no reason to feel guilt.

I thought that until I saw the sad, dark eyes of the woman who had given birth to Jamie Morales, a woman who still clearly mourned his death. In my fantasy of meeting her, I had found words to explain what had happened, to explain that at the time, when Jamie shot Curtis, I could see no other option but to shoot back. Even in retrospect, replaying the terror of the moment in my mind, I knew I had had to shoot.

131

I knew that. And guilt still hit me like a baseball bat in the back of the neck.

"I'm sorry about your son," I said. I had to steady myself against the wall.

The talk show audience screamed with muted laughter.

Elva Morales nodded. "I am sorry about your friend. How is he doing?"

"Not too well. He has pneumonia."

"I hope he's okay. His mother is with him?"

"Yes."

"Okay. Tell her I pray for her." She stood there with the dignity of a short, squat, brown-skinned goddess, an Old European earth mother, regarding me. "I got to leave. But just one thing you could maybe do for me."

"What?"

"Don't say I didn't teach Jamie that shooting people was wrong. I told him that. I had to work to put food on the table, and I told him he had to work. I told him that all the time. Somehow he got the idea that he didn't have to listen to me, that he could get things without working for them. Did you listen to everything your mother told you?"

"No. I guess I didn't."

She nodded again. "Neither did Jamie. What he did was wrong. I wish he didn't have a gun. Maybe your mother wishes you didn't have a gun, too. He had a gun. You had a gun. And I guess you did what you had to do. But I don't have to like any of it."

Elva Morales started toward me, and I instinctively stepped out of the way. She walked past me and out the front door without stopping. Elena hurried after her.

I sat down in one of the chairs, without waiting to be asked. Some actress in a commercial was getting excited about her laundry. I looked for the remote, to shut her off, but Elena came back before I found it.

"How long are you going to stay?" she asked.

"How long will it take you to tell me everything you told Mike Danken?"

"Not long." She balanced her weight against the arm of the sofa, not quite sitting. "Because Charlie didn't tell me nothing. And that's what I told Reverend Mike. I told the detective that, too, and Louise, and it's the truth."

"Did Charlie talk about his job?"

"No."

"When did he start working late on Tuesday and Thursday nights?"

"Maybe two, maybe three months ago."

"When did you complain about it?"

"When I asked him about the money, and he said he wasn't getting paid for the time."

"And he hit you?"

"Not the first time I asked. But with Christmas coming, and everybody needing stuff, I told him he shouldn't work without getting paid. And then he hit me. But it wasn't me he was angry with, I knew that. It's just he wouldn't tell me what it was."

I glanced around the room, looking for signs that it had recently been decorated, pine needles on the carpet, a sliver of dropped tinsel, a last hopeful card. Nothing.

"Did you try to find out from anybody else?"

"I asked Letty, that's all. But she didn't know either. She said he turned his truck in on time every day and left in his car. That's all she knew."

"Every day? Even with Christmas coming up?"

"That was what was weird, you know? Letty said Charlie didn't want any overtime. He said give it to somebody else."

I struggled to come up with another question.

The talk show audience was laughing again.

"Is there anyone Charlie would have confided in? A buddy?"

"No, I don't think so. I don't know. Maybe he talked to somebody at the Zanzibar."

"What?"

"Down the street. On Pyramid Way. They have a big TV. He liked to watch football, especially the San Diego Chargers."

"I'll check." The television in the living room looked big enough to me, but what do I know about football? Just an excuse for guys with muscles to hug each other.

"You seem close to your cousin Elva. Was Charlie close to Mr. Morales?"

"Who? What Mr. Morales?" She almost fell off her perch. "You mean Elva's husband? He died. And it was a long time ago. And it's none of your business, okay?"

"Okay."

"Listen, I think this is enough. I want somebody to find Reverend Mike, or I wouldn't have talked to you this much, but I think this is enough."

"Okay." I pulled out a card and placed it on the television set. "Call me if you think of anything that might help."

She didn't see me to the door.

I drove to Pyramid Way and cruised both ways until I found the Zanzibar, a sports bar identified by a sign decorated incongruously with neon palm trees, in a mini-mall with a drugstore, a coffee shop, and outlet stores for auto parts, clothing, and china. I thought about Ramona, and how distressed she was at having lost the Reno she had grown up in.

I wondered why she was so much more sentimental about it than I was. Time, age, something.

If Charlie Castro had been a football fan, Sunday afternoon would be the time to visit the Zanzibar. The afternoon of New Year's Eve. I wasn't looking forward to discovering who would willingly spend it in a bar with a large TV. Not at all.

I turned the corner and pulled into the minimall parking lot. Maybe the Friday afternoon bartender was the same guy who worked Sundays.

If he was, he had to be lonely. He and I were the only two in the bar, not counting the talk show hostess, her guests, and her audience, now considerably larger than life. I understood for the first time why television models try to get down to a size four. The red blazer the hostess wore looked big enough to cover the Statue of Liberty. Seeing yourself six feet by six feet, dwarfing the small, round tables—even dwarfing the neon palm trees—would make anybody think about dieting.

The bartender slapped a square paper napkin down and waited for me to sit in front of it. He had that ex-jock-in-a-beer-commercial look, with a gut that advertised he had always gone for better taste over less filling. Sandy hair, turning gray, cut a little too short to curl, topped a face I wouldn't want to meet across a poker table.

"A Coke'll be fine," I said.

He picked up a glass, scooped a few ice cubes into it, and filled it from one of those things that looks like a cobra head with buttons. Then he pared a narrow slice of lemon peel, ran it around the rim, and dropped it in. Only after that did he place the glass on the napkin.

"Anything else?" he asked.

"Not unless you can tell me something about a sports fan named Charlie Castro."

"Chargers fan," he corrected. "Late Chargers fan, to be precise. But that's all I know about him. That and his beer brand."

"He didn't tell you his problems?"

The guy didn't even shake his head.

"Is there anyone else he might have told?" I continued.

"Ask his wife. Ask the cops. I can't help you."

"You know he was murdered. Do you also know a friend who was asking questions about Charlie has disappeared?" I tried waiting for a reaction, then gave it up. "Did anyone else ask you about Charlie Castro?"

"Lots of people in here ask about Charlie Castro. Lots of people watched football with him. Lots of people knew him. Do you want to run a tab?"

I fished a five out of my wallet. He rang up a dollar fifty on an old cash register and placed three ones and two quarters on the counter.

"Suppose I came back on Sunday. Who would I look for?"

"Somebody who isn't afraid of trouble. Take your change."

He picked up a TV remote and flicked the volume control.

"She told you what?" the hostess shrieked.

I drank my Coke, picked up the change, and left.

I headed straight home, hoping for a message from Louise Danken, telling me Mike was there. My second choice was a message from Sandra, telling me Sierra Express was a known front for heroin smugglers.

What I got was a message from Baxter Cate.

"Call me," he said. "I won't give up until we sit down face to face."

I gave up and called.

"Back off," I said. "I can't do this. I can't talk to kids in Reno, let alone kids around the state."

"I can understand how you'd be nervous, Miss O'Neal. But I'm not going to take this as a definite refusal." He sounded rehearsed and uncomfortable, the same way he sounded on television. The same way I'd sound in front of a group of students. "I want you to think of me as a friend. And if you feel you need to take a vacation, a little paid vacation that would involve a token appearance in, say, Elko or Winnemucca, or even Las Vegas, then remember my phone number. All right?"

I wanted to say something rude. Instead I hung up in his ear.

The case of the deadbeat dad was still dangling, but I couldn't think of a new direction. Besides, I was hooked on the Morales/Castro/Danken situation. I booted up my computer and trolled the Internet for the next couple of hours, hoping to come up with something more useful than Elva Morales's credit rating, which was good. The woman paid her bills.

When the sun had set, Sandra hadn't called, Louise hadn't called, and I was bored with scrolling through public records, I gave up on the Internet, fed the cats, and walked to the Mother Lode.

Diane opened a beer when she saw me heading for the counter.

"Rough day?" she asked when I sat down on my usual stool.

"Rough week," I answered.

"How's Curtis?"

"Pneumonia."

"I'm sorry." She shook her head. "It could have been worse, though. The bullet could have hit his spine, and he could have been paralyzed for life."

"Yeah. Thanks."

I was halfway through the beer when Deke arrived. It didn't take long to bring him up to speed.

"You think the bartender really knows something?" he asked.

"Hard to tell. The bartender, Joe Kovanda, Letty Rashad,

Elena Castro, Elva Morales . . . any one—or all—of them could know something. Even Louise Danken could know something without understanding what she knows. Unless I can ask the right question, I'll never get the right answer."

"Best you sit back and wait for Matthews, then."

"Shit. I can't. I promised."

"Usually I'd agree. But sometimes the best of us have to break promises, and this is one of those times."

"Why?"

"Because Matthews don't want to find his friend Danken dead no more than you do. And if somebody took Danken out, that somebody won't hesitate to take you out, too. But he might hesitate over a cop."

"You think Mike Danken is dead."

"You want another beer?"

"I guess so."

Deke waved, and Diane brought another beer for me. She refilled Deke's coffee with her other hand.

"You think Mike Danken is alive?" he asked.

"No. I think I'm playing out a dead man's hand."

"Then best you sit with your friend Curtis, and take your mother to lunch, and catch up on your other clients. You don't want to be dead, too."

"What if I get another idea?"

"What other idea?"

I didn't have an answer. Deke ate his steak and I ate my hamburger—my second of the day—and I didn't have an answer.

I still didn't have an answer when I walked home and crawled into bed. I turned on the television and flicked from one channel to the next, hoping for a movie I wouldn't mind watching again.

What I found was Baxter Cate in front of a gun case. Not

that I hadn't seen the commercial before. I just hadn't noticed his belt buckle before, the one with the gold circle inside the star.

I watched to the end, trying to decipher some kind of code from the advertised prices.

When Lane Josten came on, reading copy off the Tele-PrompTer on terrorist activity in the Middle East, I turned off the set.

I had a new idea. I just had to find out what it was.

Chapter
13

LIBERTY GUN WORKS turned out to be a deep, narrow store wedged between an equally narrow pawn shop and a casino on Virginia Street, a couple of blocks north of the river. The casino seemed to have sprouted in the last week, complete with a sign that flashed alternately red, yellow, and green, doing its best to make you stop, hesitate, then come on in. Neither the gun store nor the pawn shop made a similar effort. As if the owners figured you'd come in if you needed to, wouldn't if you didn't, no matter what they did. Baxter Cate's commercials were probably even newer than the casino.

I had decided to walk rather than drive, partly because the morning was still mostly clear—the clouds in the northwest were closer, but they hadn't dropped anything yet—and partly because the downtown streets were torn up so much of the time. One casino would close and another open, the construction blocking one lane of traffic and trucks another, and what used to be a simple trip required navigating an obstacle course.

Walking, I couldn't help noticing the lettering on the old

Granada Theater's marquee: THE END OF AN ER, it said. I suspected an A had disappeared. The rest of the announcement would disappear, too, one letter at a time, and then the movie theater would be something else, a casino or a factory outlet store or something like that.

And I sort of hoped the sign disappeared before Ramona could see it. The era it referred to was the one she thought of as hers, the one in which she had seen Piper Laurie and Tony Curtis shooting a movie in front of Woolworth's, a movie that would later play at the Granada Theater, or the Crest, or the Majestic, all closed. She knew the era was over, but seeing it crumble on the marquee wouldn't make her feel any better about it.

Tuesday might be a good day to take her to lunch. January second. If Curtis were well enough—Curtis would be well enough—and the weather held, maybe Ramona and Tola Rae and I could have lunch at the French place on South Virginia that Ramona kept talking about. If she ever remembered the name, and if it hadn't been sold again.

When I reached the glass door to Liberty Gun Works, I discovered one more way in which it was less inviting than its next door neighbor the casino. I had to ring for entrance. A man behind a counter looked at me carefully before he hit a buzzer to release the lock and let me in.

"Is Baxter Cate here?" I asked.

The door clicked behind me.

"He doesn't always come in on Saturdays, Miss O'Neal, but it doesn't take him long to get here. Why don't you take a look around the store? You might see something you like. I'll give him a call. I know he'd like to wait on you personally. Although I'd be happy to do that myself. So if you want something taken out of a case before he gets here, just ask." The words came out in yaps, like a lap dog dying to please.

Not that the man was that small. He was probably five foot six or so, but thin, with the gray hair, glasses, and eager smile of an aging, overworked postal worker who knows he is about to get the ax.

I probably shouldn't have been surprised that he knew my name. Or that he thought me a likely customer. But I still had a moment of sheer terror, hoping I wasn't locked into an enclosed space with someone who might suddenly reach for a gun, with plenty to choose from.

I also checked his clothes. Plaid shirt, jeans held up by a worn leather belt sporting the simple buckle it had been made with. Nothing special.

"Thanks," I said, with what I hoped was a pleasant nod. "I'd appreciate it if you'd let Baxter know I'm here."

Most of the time, dropping in on people unannounced gives me an edge in the interrogation. But it doesn't always work out the way I want. I looked around the store as he punched a number into a cordless phone and whispered something to whoever answered.

Guns. Guns in racks and guns in cases, one of which was the backdrop for Baxter Cate's commercial. Small arms, semiautomatics, rifles, shotguns, everything for the sports minded, some for the military minded as well. Billy the Kid would have let out a whoop and a holler.

So would the Clantons—the family who died at the O.K. Corral rather than set their guns aside before going into town. And that was what bothered me. This store was smack in the middle of downtown Reno. Wyatt Earp had it right, I think. Guns belong outside the city.

I say that, and I know we can't set up metal detectors at the city limits. Move Liberty Gun Works a couple of miles south, and the difference is only symbolic. Hell, move it to Arizona. The guns get to the city all the same.

"I heard it was an All American .22 you used on that criminal in the mall."

I jerked around.

"I'm Morris Gandy." He held out his hand, and I shook it. His skin was warm and dry. "That was fine shooting, with a .22, but you know that. A lesser marksman—or markswoman, I should say—would have missed. One shot. My God, one shot."

I retrieved my hand.

"Normally I'd try to sell you on something a little more powerful, but I guess you don't need it. See anything you like, though, I'll get it out of the case."

"I use a nine millimeter Beretta for target practice," I said, and immediately regretted volunteering the information.

"Hey, where do you go? Baxter's going to be opening up a new range west of the city, where the old Lawton Hot Springs used to be. Sort of like a country club, he says. Dining room, bar, dance floor, with target shooting instead of golf."

"Sounds like fun." I tried to smile. "Listen, I don't want to take up your time. Why don't I go run a couple of errands and come back when Baxter's here?"

"No need. Baxter'll be here any minute. His wife said he'd left the house a while ago."

"Well, then he'll have to wait for me." I pulled the gift certificate from Ramona out of my pocket, waved it at him, and took a couple of sideways steps toward the door. "Let him know I'm just up the street, trying on new boots. Late Christmas present."

"No need. Really. He's on his way." His smile didn't waver, and his hands stayed on the counter.

I was trying to figure out a way to strengthen my

argument when the bell sounded. The man turned, nodded, and pressed the buzzer.

Baxter Cate walked in. The door clicked shut behind him.

"Miss O'Neal!" He grabbed my hand and pumped it.

"Mr. Cate." I was actually glad to see him.

"Awright. We'll make it Freddie and Baxter. A very, very pleasant surprise, finding you here. Very pleasant. I hope you haven't been waiting long. Has Morris kept you entertained? How about coffee?"

Cate had in person and without makeup the same claymation look that he had on television. Part of it was the contrast between dyed black hair—or what I could see of it peeking out from under a Stetson—and thin cheeks that sagged into a receding double chin, part the porcelain teeth. Mostly it was the eyes that twinkled with a life of their own, whatever was going on with the sagging flesh.

"I didn't think to offer her coffee," Morris said. "But it's made, in the office."

"Come on back." Cate wasn't much taller than Morris, but the hat brought him up to average. He slipped past me and walked with an exaggerated, bowlegged swagger down the narrow corridor between the counter and the cases to a door marked Private.

I stifled my claustrophobia and followed him into a room barely large enough to accommodate a desk and two chairs. Most of the desk space was taken up by an automatic coffee machine and a computer. An open door on the left wall led to a closet with a toilet. Cate closed the door behind us, then the one that hid the toilet, nodding in embarrassment, and pointed to the chair beside the desk.

"I hope you take your coffee black," he said.

"That's fine."

He pulled one white foam cup and one white mug out of

a drawer and filled both. The mug had a gold circle inside a star on one side and the number 601 on the other.

Cate handed me the foam cup and took his seat.

"I'm so glad you reconsidered," he said. "Saved me a lot more phone calls, because I wasn't giving up."

"I still don't think I'm the right person to make speeches to high school students."

"'Course you are. We'll videotape a reenactment of the scene in the parking lot, with you playing yourself and actors taking the other parts. Scare the hell out of those kids. Or most of them, anyway."

"Scare the hell out of their teachers and their parents, too. And maybe give them the wrong idea about the role of private citizens in law enforcement."

"Now, Freddie, you must know that in this state private citizens have always felt they have a role in law enforcement."

"I'm not sure what you mean by that, sir."

"Baxter."

"Right."

"What I mean by that is Reno has always attracted a certain undesirable element, and sometimes private citizens have done a better job than the law in seeing that they don't feel welcome."

"What do you mean by 'undesirable element'?"

"Well, that sort of changes with the times, doesn't it? Back in the nineteenth century it was the Chinese, of course. Did you know they worked on the railroad for a dollar a day when the Irish got two?"

"I did. That's where the expression 'coolie wages' came from. I heard it the first time I took a job, when I was a teenager." I took a sip of coffee. It was thick and lukewarm. Morris must have made the pot before he opened the store, whatever time that was. "But the Chinese worked for their money, and they were law-abiding. I'm not sure what made them an undesirable element."

"Looking at it now, it's maybe not so clear-cut. Besides, the Chinese are good gamblers, and some of them have a lot of money. But it seemed different at the time. And there were other undesirables, the horse thieves and the claim jumpers and the highwaymen." He waved off the objection he saw coming, about the leap from the Chinese to the horse thieves. "The law couldn't always move. And that's still true. Take your own case. The law couldn't have moved in that parking lot, not fast enough to save you. Wouldn't it have been better if that whole family had been run out of town before any of this happened?"

I shifted in the uncomfortable folding chair. "I might have thought so a week ago. Since then, I've met a couple of family members who seem all right to me."

"Well, you might not want to get too involved with them, Freddie." His tone was one he might use with a daughter. Not a good choice.

"Why not?" I kept my voice level. It wasn't easy.

"You're a smart girl, and you have a good reputation as a detective. Find out the story of the senior Morales, George Morales, and we'll talk again. That may convince you I'm right."

"You don't want to tell me?"

He tittered with laughter, and then had to clap his hand to his mouth when his teeth shook.

"I think the tale will mean more if it comes from someone else."

"Okay. I'll do that. But that's going to take some time, and right now I'm a little worried about what's going on with someone else who took an interest in the family. The Reverend Mike Danken. You know him?"

"Of course. The pastor of that little church by the park,

near the hospital. Former police officer. And one who understands that sometimes the police may need a little help. I don't think you need to worry about him."

I closed my eyes and counted to ten. "Does that mean you have him and he's all right?"

"I have him?"

Cate paused so long that I had to open my eyes and look at him. His eyebrows were raised for dramatic effect.

"Or somebody," I said. "Whoever you represent."

"I don't represent anybody but myself, an ordinary private citizen. And I didn't know anyone was keeping the Reverend Danken against his will. If you'd like, I'll ask around and see what I can find out."

"Thanks." I placed the foam cup on the desk, resisting the urge to dump the coffee onto his keyboard. "And just one more thing. I'm really fascinated by your belt buckle. I was on my way up the street to buy some boots. Do you think I could find something like that in the store?"

I waved the gift certificate to show I was serious.

Cate tittered again. "You might, I don't know. Depends on who's there. But if you want one, I'll give you one. I'll have it here, whenever you come by for it, as long as you've found out the story of the Morales family. The full story."

"I'll see you then."

I didn't wait for him to open the office door.

"See you soon, Morris," I said, hurrying past the counter with as bright a smile as I could muster.

"I hope so, Freddie. Let me know if you want company the next time you go to the range." He pressed the buzzer and let me out, smiling his deranged postal worker smile in return.

I stood on the sidewalk and took a deep breath, relieved to be out in the cool air.

I tucked the gift certificate back into my pocket. The

boots would have to wait until I made some inquiries about George Morales.

Cate certainly had some interest in the family—both families, Morales and Castro. That was evidently why he had called me in the first place. After I shot Jamie, he figured me for an instant friend. Then I stayed involved because of Danken, and he wasn't sure whose side I was on. So he kept calling. And he still wasn't sure.

But he didn't seem to think Mike Danken was dead. For the first time since Louise called to let me know Mike was missing, I began to hope he might be alive.

There was a slight—a very slight—possibility I could get Matthews to check the police computer for something on George Morales, if I could think of an excuse for asking that wouldn't tip him off I was back on the Castro case.

The second best place to start looking for a story on George Morales was the *Herald*'s files. Sandra had never gotten back to me about Sierra Express, and it had finally hit me that "away from her desk" on the Friday before the three-day New Year weekend might mean that she had left early. If she had ever returned from the three-day Christmas weekend. I couldn't remember what she had said about that, just something about parents and in-laws.

Elena Castro had already told me that George Morales was none of my business, and I was certain her cousin would feel the same way. All I could do for the moment was try to finish my conversation with Letty Rashad.

She might be more receptive if found her away from the office, away from her boss.

I walked home to see if I could find her address. Worst case, I knew her parents lived next door to the Castros. I could go back to Sparks and stake out the street until she came to visit. That would use up the weekend in a hurry.

As it turned out, L. Rashad was listed in the telephone

directory, on Plumas Street. Too far to walk, even on a pleasant day, and the clouds had been closing in as I left the Liberty Gun Works. I took the Jeep.

The address I wanted belonged to a building in one of those apartment complexes built to give residents the illusion of privacy—lots of jutting angles to make it difficult for people to look in their neighbors' windows, and scattered trees that would make the job close to impossible in every season but the one we were now in. Nevertheless the complex itself was large enough, including six buildings, each with eight apartments, that some sense of community was inescapable.

The complex was new, vaguely Southwestern, with stuccoed walls painted the color of adobe and deep red tile roofs. And the area was pricy. I hadn't checked the rents, but I would have guessed they were out of range for somebody just out of community college who worked for a delivery service.

The bank of mailboxes showed numbers only, no names.

I found Letty's red Toyota in a carport with eight slots and tried to come up with a pattern that would link it to one of the eight apartments in the building. A logical way to assign them was to start with ground floor, near side, and go from there. That would place Letty on the second floor. I'd have to guess near side or far side. I started with the near side.

And Letty answered my knock.

"What are you doing here? How did you find me?"

She only opened the door as far as a chain lock would allow. I caught a glimpse of dark hair, a red silk robe, and one frightened dark eye.

"I found you from the telephone directory. I'm here to finish our conversation."

"Oh, God. I can't talk to you."

"Why not? You're a friend of the Castro family, and you

know all I'm trying to do is follow up on what happened to Mike Danken when he was looking into what happened to Charlie. I have no other interest in this." I did my best to look harmless.

"Who is it?" a man's voice called from behind her.

"Wrong door. I'll be right there," she answered, then turned back to me. "Please go away. Please. If you go away, I'll call when I can."

"Is something wrong?" the voice asked.

"No. I'm just giving directions, Joey, it's all right. Please," she added, either to him or to me.

"Okay," I said, backing away. "But I hope that's a promise, to call me."

She closed the door in my face.

I was sorry I hadn't gotten a look at Joey, just to check his belt buckle.

I drove home. I thought about stopping by Washoe Medical to see Curtis, but when I had called in the morning, Tola Rae hadn't sounded encouraging. She'd said the painkillers and the antibiotics were keeping him drowsy. I decided to give him until the next day. I could check in on my way to watch football at the Zanzibar, which was the only useful thing I could do before Tuesday, unless Letty actually called.

When I got back to my office, I called Louise Danken, just to let her know that I was doing my best, even though I had nothing to report. She sounded so forlorn that I added, "Please don't give up. There's a good chance that he's going to turn up unharmed."

"What do you know that you didn't know yesterday?" she asked, her voice suddenly hard and alert.

"Nothing. Really. Just a hunch. I'll tell you when it's something."

"You're going down the same path Mike did, aren't you?"

"I don't know."

"Be sure to let someone know where you're going before you disappear."

"I don't plan on disappearing, Louise. If I go anywhere chancy, I'll leave word. I promise."

"What if you don't know it's chancy?"

"Do you want me to follow up on this or not?" I was getting irritated. I didn't need to be reminded that somebody out there was a murderer.

She was silent for a moment. "I want you to do this. Thank you. Please be careful. And call me any time."

I hung up the phone and reached for the directory.

I looked up L. Rashad for a second time, then found the number in the reverse directory. I had been hoping to find a second name, and there it was. Letty's roommate was Joseph Kovanda, Jr.

Chapter 14

THE ZANZIBAR ON the Sunday afternoon of New Year's Eve might have looked like a fun place to be if I were watching it from the cool distance of television. Up close and personal, the ambience was loud, crowded, and reeking with the sad odor of desperation. The bar was evidently the last stop for those without a New Year's Eve date, both male and female, as well as a starting place for those who didn't want to face their evening companions sober.

One of the lesser Bowls was being played out on the large screen, with giant twenty-year-olds in red jerseys opposing their counterparts in white. I couldn't tell whether the announcers had been muted or the babble from the patrons had simply overcome them, one aimless chatter scoring, the other not. Scattered cheers from the watchers and a soft roar from the television marked a touchdown for the team in white, which appeared to be the underdog.

Because Elena had indicated that Charlie came to the bar without her, I had been braced for some kind of men's club. I was surprised by the number of women, the number of young, pretty women—pretty is a limp word, but it's the right choice—who were laughing in clusters around the small tables, or interspersed among the men at the bar.

The mixed crowd made being there easier in one sense. I didn't stand out the way I'd feared I might. But trying to talk to someone—anyone—was going to be complicated by the nature of the other conversations between men and women who hadn't been formally introduced. I wasn't looking for a date for the night.

I had checked on Curtis before leaving the house. Tola Rae said he was doing better, and I said I'd stop by on my way home. I had seen enough New Years in with Jay Leno—and Johnny Carson before him—that one more wasn't going to bother me.

The canned sardine nature of the Zanzibar did.

If the bartender remembered me, he managed not to show it. Unless serving people who elbowed their way in next to me four times before asking for my order counted. I didn't attempt a question about possible Chargers fans. I didn't tip him, either.

I turned around, leaning my back against the bar, and assessed the room. Charlie Castro had been a regular, so someone here had known him. I watched the ebb and flow from table to bar and back as the two waitresses became increasingly unable to handle the rate of consumption.

I was on my second beer before the pecking order among the primates became clear.

A table of six men, no women, positioned before the center of the large screen, but far enough back to avoid distortion, had the consistent attention of one waitress. No one had to do more than raise an empty bottle of beer to have it immediately replaced. They were there to watch the game, and to get drunk doing it. Without their wives. I noted wedding rings on two raised hands, and there could have been others.

All six seemed to be in their late thirties to early forties, blue-collar working types of indeterminate ethnicity, somewhere between Hispanic and non-Hispanic white. They had an insularity from their surroundings that seemed to come from long familiarity. Like fish in water, they took the atmosphere in through gills and let it out again without thinking about it.

A low-level rowdiness would erupt between plays, then subside, although one of the men wasn't rising to the occasion. He didn't even respond to the shoulder punches designed to jolt him out of his sulk.

I waited for halftime before approaching the table.

"If there's a Chargers fan in the crowd, I'd like to buy him a beer," I said, moving between the silent man and his most persistent puncher.

Five of them assessed me. The silent man answered without looking around.

"We're all Chargers fans. But we buy our own beer."

"I saw her on television," the man on the other side of him said. "She carries a gun in her boot. Used it to shoot the teenager in the mall parking lot. You carrying your gun in your boot?"

"Not today," I replied. Damn all television coverage of crime to hell.

"I would have picked you for a 'Niners fan," another one said. "Or Raiders. Not Chargers. I'll bet you can't even tell us who the quarterback is."

"Doesn't mean I wouldn't buy you a drink," I said.

"We buy our own."

I had to stop thinking of him as the silent man, since he obviously talked. He shifted so that he could look at me. He had a fleshy face under thinning brown hair, a nose starting to bloom with broken veins, and eyes that had trouble deciding which part of the thick bifocals to use. One heavy

forearm was braced against the table, the other on the back
of the chair.

"Not because you shot the Morales kid," he continued. "If
anybody needed shooting, he did. But this is a private
gathering, even if it's in a public place. There's no room for
you at this table."

"We have a difference of opinion about Jamie Morales,
my friend," said another of the men. "But that is for another
time. For now, we agree. There is no room for this woman
at this table."

"Don't make us call Mack," the man with the forearms
and glasses said, nodding in the direction of the bar.

I glanced over. The bartender knew what was going on.
His eyes swept the room as he filled the tilted glasses from
the beer taps. They paused to meet mine only long enough
to let me know I was in trouble if I stayed.

A strategic retreat was in order. I pulled out a few
business cards and dropped them on the table, hoping they'd
land in a dry spot.

"The offer of a beer stays open," I said.

As if on cue, they all turned their attention back to the
oversized screen, just in time to catch a fashion ad that could
have been a nightmare sequence in an Italian movie. It had
to have been lost on this crowd. A few of the women at the
bar were still young enough and skinny enough to wear the
clothes. But I'd give ten-to-one odds that they all bought
their nondesigner blue jeans at the outlet store down the
block. Brand loyalty for beer. Plain wrap for denim.

I worked my way to the door, grateful to breathe the cool
air. A few flakes of snow drifted into my face as I walked to
the Jeep. I wasn't ready to go home. I wasn't even ready to
visit Curtis.

I decided to see if I couldn't apply a little pressure on

Letty Rashad. Her parents lived next door to Elena Castro. I had a fifty-fifty chance of knocking on the right door.

The bet settled in my favor before I got out of the car. A young man on his way from the Castro front door to a dented, white Ford Escort stopped to call a greeting to a woman carrying groceries into the house on the left. The thick, wild gray hair marked her as a member of Letty's gene pool.

I stayed in the car until the Castro boy had driven away. I had parked shy of the Castro house, and I hoped I could make it across the lawn before Elena spotted me.

In that, I was lucky. Or at least she didn't come running out to confront me. I made it to the porch and rang the bell.

The woman with the wild gray hair opened the door.

"Oh, God," she said. "You."

"We haven't met, Mrs. Rashad," I responded weakly.

"You shot Jamie, you found Charlie murdered, you hassled Letty and Elena, you slandered Elva on television, what do you want with me?" She had also given Letty her creamed chocolate skin and black eyes. The firm chin was her own.

"I shot Jamie because I didn't have a choice. And all I want with you is a chance to talk about the rest of it. If Charlie Castro was murdered because of something going on at Sierra Express—and I don't know that he was—but if he was, then Letty may be in danger. I hoped that if I could talk to you, you would talk to her."

"And tell her what? That Joey Kovanda is going to mess up her life?"

"Well, to start with."

"I told her that. And what else?"

She hadn't touched the screen door. It was cold on the porch, and the snowflakes were drifting a little closer together, but I didn't ask her to let me in.

"If she knows anything about why Charlie Castro was murdered, her association with the Kovandas may do more than mess up her life."

"You're fishing, right?"

"Right. I am. For a good reason. I need to find out where Mike Danken is before something happens to him."

"I can't help you." She started to close the door.

"Wait a minute, damn it, because if you don't help me, I may take it out on Robert."

That came out before I thought about it, but it worked. She opened the door again.

"What do you mean?"

"I agreed to probation. If I change my mind, I can make things tough for him." I wasn't certain about that, but I knew I could make the news with it. If I ever wanted to make the news about anything ever again, which I didn't.

"Why would you change your mind?"

"I need to find Mike Danken. I am running out of people who might be able to help. If Letty can help, I need whatever information she has, and if the only way I can get it is to threaten Robert Morales, I will. Is that clear?"

She nodded. "Okay. I'll tell her."

"And tell her to listen. And while I'm asking for help, I need to know the story of the Morales family. What happened to George Morales?"

"I can't tell you that. And threats won't help. I don't know what happened to Elva's husband. But I'll tell you one thing. Threatening Robert is mean, no matter why you're doing it. It's mean."

A door was shut in my face one more time.

I didn't know Robert Morales, but I remembered the fear in his face, probably a mirror of the fear in my own. And threatening Robert felt mean. It felt so mean that I wasn't going to do it again if I could find any other way to get his father's story, or if I could find any other way to Mike Danken, other than Baxter Cate.

I was ready to go home. But I had promised to stop by the hospital.

The snow flurries were beating on the windshield by the time I reached the Washoe Medical parking lot. I could barely see the man in the information booth as I passed.

The Christmas tree was still up. I hurried to the elevators, shaking snow off my sheepskin jacket before it could melt and soak in.

Curtis was looking a little better. The oxygen mask was gone, replaced by the split tube to the nostrils.

Tola Rae ducked out for coffee, and I sat on the edge of the bed.

"How're you doing?" I asked.

"Tired. You?"

"Tired. Looking for Mike Danken is like staring at a maze. There are several paths, most of which will be dead ends, one of which will take me home. I'm looking forward to home."

Curtis nodded and turned toward the window.

"I'm sorry," I added. "Do you have any idea yet how long you'll be here?"

"Not much longer. The doctor says that I should leave within the next day or so, as long as I have someone to take care of me."

I had a sinking feeling as I heard that.

"Well, you do, don't you? I thought Tola Rae was going to be here indefinitely."

"She can't do it alone."

"No, but it shouldn't be hard to find a licensed nurse to help her."

He was still turned toward the window. Nothing to see out there but snowflakes.

"She thought I might want to go back to Richmond for a few weeks. In Richmond, she already has help," he whispered. "Alan has released me from classes for the spring semester, and the Channel 12 consulting job is mostly taken care of. Recuperating might be easier in a warmer climate."

"Yes. And it isn't just the cold. There's the problem of the wood smoke, too. Not even good for healthy lungs." My heart was curling in on itself as I said it.

"This isn't decided," he whispered. "And it would only be for a few weeks at most."

I thought I was going to gut it out. I intended to gut it out. I opened my mouth, planning to say something more about how Virginia might be good for him, and we could talk on the phone and send e-mail while he was gone. But nothing came out. I leaned forward, put my forehead against his chest, and began to sob. Awful, heart-wrenching sobs, coming from the base of whatever defined me as a person.

He shifted my head to his shoulder.

"I'm not leaving you," he whispered. "I promise. Going to Virginia to heal isn't leaving you."

I wanted to tell him I knew that. All I could do was cry. For a moment, I didn't think I was going to stop crying, ever. But I did.

We were lying there in silence when Tola Rae returned.

"I could get another cup of coffee, if you like," she said.

"That's okay." I sat up and rubbed my eyes, hoping to create an excuse for the redness. "I ought to get going."

"I've convinced the doctor that one glass of wine on New Year's Eve would have no ill effects on the patient. Why don't you come back about seven?"

I struggled with that, wondering what we were going to be drinking to.

"Fine. I'll see you then. And thank you for asking me." In

truth, I wasn't certain whether I could bring myself to come back.

"Please come back," Curtis whispered. He must have picked up the edge in my voice.

"I will. But I won't be able to stay too long—I'm having dinner with Deke." I hated the half lie even as I said it. I would have dinner with Deke, though. I'd make it true.

I felt it was one more retreat, and at least one too many that day, as I left the room and headed down in the elevator.

Outside, the snow had formed a thin white layer on shrubs and benches. The constant fall was just heavy enough to obscure vision. I drove home carefully. If it kept up like that, I might have an excuse to stay home.

I called Louise Danken, just to let her know I was still on the case.

She sounded subdued as she thanked me for checking in so faithfully. I had nothing to say that would cheer her up, so I got off the phone as quickly as I could.

Then I left a message for Deke, that I'd be at the Mother Lode at eight.

Having covered myself, I lay down on the bed to regroup my forces. The cats were on me in two bounds, Butch on my stomach and Sundance on my shoulder. It took a hand on each, keeping them separate, to get them settled down.

And I stayed like that, flat on my back with the cats on top of me, until it was time to go back to the hospital. I had no new strength, no new insight, no new anything. But the snow had stopped, so I had no excuse, either.

The drink at the hospital was difficult. I suppose the wine was good, but it was wasted on me. Curtis didn't talk, I didn't talk, and Tola Rae chattered on about the New Year's Eve party at the house when Curtis was fourteen, and how he had slipped a champagne bottle out of the refrigerator without anyone noticing. She found him on the bathroom floor, praying to the porcelain gods. And another New Year's Eve party where Curtis did something. And another. And I had to leave.

I had walked to the hospital, not wanting to risk driving on New Year's Eve with all the idiots on the road. The walk to the Mother Lode was a little chillier than I was ready for, but that was all right. At least I knew my blood was flowing.

Deke was waiting for me at the counter.

"I didn't know we had a date," he said.

"If you had other plans, you could have called me back."

A young woman I hadn't seen before brought me a beer. She had what appeared to be very long black hair wrapped up tightly under a waitress's cap.

"Where's Diane?" I asked.

"On vacation for two weeks, starting today," she answered. "But she left me notes on the regulars."

"And your name is . . . ?"

"Sarah. Sarah Urrutia."

"Have any relatives in law enforcement?"

"Oh, lots." She giggled, and I hoped someone had checked her age before hiring her. "My sister Michelle is a police officer here in Reno, and my cousin Kenny is police chief in Elko, and—"

"That's enough," I said.

"But my great-grandfather was a sheriff." She sounded hurt that I'd cut her off.

"I didn't know that. Thanks for telling me."

"Anything else?"

"A hamburger for me, whatever Deke wants for him. No hurry."

"A steak for Deke," she said, her face brightening, and hurried off to place the order, even though I'd told her not to.

"Now," Deke said. "About our date."

"I didn't want to stay at the hospital. And I didn't want to lie about where I was going."

"Shouldn't your friend Curtis be about out of there? Bullet wounds be dicey, especially when central organs are involved. But unless there is something funny with the insurance going on, they ought to be about sending him home."

"Yeah, they are. But Tola Rae thinks home is Richmond, and it looks like he might be going with her."

"Not for good. He has a job here—I'm not going to say he has you. He has a job here and a life here."

"I know. I do know. But I just feel this is all some kind of disaster, spiraling downward, and Curtis leaving is one more turn of the screw."

"What else?"

I brought him up to date on the events of the last couple of days.

"And the thing is, I do feel mean about threatening Robert—Mrs. Rashad was right. And I just don't know how much more I can do," I finished.

"Right now, you don't know if it will come to threatening Robert," Deke said. He paused while Sarah Urrutia delivered our plates, then continued. "You got a couple of possible leads on Sierra Express. Sandra may come through about Morales. Hell, one of them boys from the bar might come through about Morales. Your buddy Matthews won't. But he may break the case without you. So eat your hamburger and don't worry about threatening Robert or finding Danken and just be grateful that tomorrow is another year."

I almost said something about Scarlett O'Hara, but I wasn't sure Deke had seen the movie, or liked it if he had.

I started in on my hamburger, grateful that at least I had a friend.

"Another beer?" Sarah Urrutia asked.

"No, just the check. And when you talk to your cousin Kenny, tell him I said Happy New Year."

Sarah looked startled, and Deke chuckled.

"A story for another time," he told her. "But you could call and tell him yourself," he added to me.

"Another time," I said.

Feeling nostalgic for something that happened is bad enough. Feeling nostalgic for something that didn't happen wouldn't help my evening. And calling Kenny Urrutia because I was afraid Curtis might leave me wouldn't help anything.

Deke, the cats, and Jay Leno. And I made it through the New Year ceremony, one more time.

Chapter
15

A "TWILIGHT ZONE" marathon and a pizza delivery saw me through New Year's Day. I had intended to rent a half dozen videotapes, but life had gotten in the way, and the store was closed for the holiday. It had been awhile since I had watched the old half hour episodes, and I was pleasantly surprised at how well they held up, even with an extra five minutes of commercials.

By Tuesday, I was sick of my own funk. I called Sandra first thing in the morning.

"I just got in," she said. "And I just got your message. What is it you need?"

"Anything you have on Sierra Express or its owner, Joe Kovanda, and anything you have on George Morales."

"George?"

"Jamie's father. And just for the hell of it, anything you have on Mike Danken."

"The man with the church in his house?"

"Yeah. He's been missing for almost a week."

"I'm sorry. I really needed the vacation, though, and I didn't watch the news. Why are you involved?"

"Because I said I'd back him up if he got into trouble, and his wife believed it. I'm glad you had a good vacation." I meant it. Really. I was barely envious that somebody else's life was fine.

"I did invite you."

"I know. And I did what I wanted to do."

"All right. Sierra Express, Joe Kovanda, George Morales, Mike Danken. Anybody else?"

I thought of adding Baxter Cate, but I heard the touch of sarcasm in her voice.

"No, that's enough. And I'll buy lunch, if you can check this stuff out by then."

"I think I can justify spending the morning doing background on Danken's disappearance, unless someone else has the story."

"I don't think anybody else really knows it's a story. Louise—his wife—hasn't talked to the media, as far as I know. And I don't think most people, even most reporters, would connect Danken with Charlie Castro."

" 'Curiouser and curiouser.' I'll meet you at noon at Harrah's, even if I have to bully an intern into helping me look through computer files. How's Curtis?"

"Better. More at noon."

I didn't want to tell her over the phone that he was going to Virginia. I didn't want to tell her at all. I had managed to stop feeling sorry for myself, and I didn't want to start all over again.

I thought about calling Matthews. I had tried, in the insomniac hours of the morning, to come up with a reason to ask him about George Morales that didn't include looking for Danken. I couldn't find one. And worst case, I would then have let him know I was looking, and George Morales wouldn't be in the police computer anyway.

I decided to wait. I could call Matthews when I had something to tell him.

And nobody had called me by the time I walked out the door, heading for a brief stop at the hospital, then lunch with Sandra.

The storm had moved on, and the day was crisp and white and hopeful.

Curtis was even out of bed and looking better.

But the meeting was awkward, and I wanted to escape. He had decided to go to Virginia, I knew that was coming, and he didn't want me to cry anymore. And Tola Rae didn't go for coffee.

The day didn't seem quite as bright as I retraced my way down Mill toward Virginia.

Sandra was waiting in a corner booth when I arrived at the coffee shop.

"Bad news?" she asked. "You look more depressed than you sounded over the phone."

She looked rested and relaxed and ready to work. For an instant, I was unreasonably pissed at her.

"Not really. Curtis is doing fine, and he thinks he'll be even finer in Virginia for a while. And he's right. He'll have a better climate and better care—Tola Rae and the servants. It's the thing to do."

She barely blinked. "It is the thing to do. He does need care, and you can't do it. And he'll come back."

"That's what Deke said. And I know I can't take care of him. I can't even stand to stay in the hospital for more than about fifteen minutes. And I wouldn't have the patience or the skill to provide everything he'll need for his convalescence. Which will take time. Gunshots take time to heal." I bit my lip to stop talking.

Sandra sighed. "I'm about to give advice. Every once in a while, I have an impulse to do that, and the impulse overpowers me more and more often since I've become a mother. Ready?"

"Ready." I forced a smile, which is what she really wanted.

"Let him go and don't worry about it. Take care of what's in front of you, concentrate on that, let him concentrate on healing. If he hasn't come back to Reno by the time you're ready to concentrate on him, fly to Richmond. How's that?"

"Pretty good. I'm not sure I can actually control the worry part, but I'll do my best on the concentration. Did your search through the computer files turn up anything that will help?"

"I think so. Let's start with Mike Danken, ex-cop turned minister of his own church. He's actually an ordained minister of the Universal Life Church."

"You mean he's a minister because he has one of those mail-order certificates? The kind you can get for ten dollars if a friend wants you to perform a wedding? That's what he has?"

"That's all. We did a story on him six years ago when he retired from the police force after twenty years—officer-involved shooting, his second. And this is what will really catch your attention. The first man he killed was George Morales."

"You're right. You have my attention."

"Danken was vindicated. Morales shot first. He was vindicated the second time, too. But Danken said the experience of taking a life brought home to him how fragile life is, and so on. And when he had to shoot a second time, he realized he might have to shoot a third and a fourth, and he didn't like the person he might become. It's all in here." She held up a folder that had been lying on the table. "He said he didn't have time to go back to school, had to get straight to his new task, which was helping people who were the victims of violence, no matter which side of the gun they were on."

That made a little more sense of my encounter with him. "How does he make it financially, I wonder, if he's not part of a real church. I can't imagine that a collection plate in his living room covers the rent, even with his police pension."

"I can't help you with that."

"So what did Morales do?"

"Stuck up a convenience store. Shot the clerk. Danken was off-duty, but he had his gun. It was twelve years ago. I copied that article for you, too."

I wondered if Jamie had shot Curtis with his daddy's gun.

"And Sierra Express?" I asked.

"A member of good standing of the Reno Chamber of Commerce as far as the *Herald* is concerned. The only reference to Joe Kovanda I could find was a quote on business picking up when the recession was over. I didn't think you'd want it."

"No, that's okay."

"What did you think you'd find?"

"I don't want to interrupt," a waitress said, "but I'll be happy to take your order whenever you're ready."

"We'll order," Sandra said. "Two chicken salads. Thank you."

"Suppose I didn't want a chicken salad?" I said, after the waitress had scribbled something on her pad and walked away.

"We're taking up a table at lunch, and she had been watching us ever since you sat down. I wanted to spare her the menu reading."

"Great. Next time I'll order for you."

"Fine. So what did you want on Sierra Express?"

"A reason why Charlie Castro's body might be left there. It had to be a warning to somebody, about something. You said they belong to the Chamber of Commerce. I don't suppose the Chamber is selling belt buckles, a gold circle inside a silver star."

"Not that I know of. Why?"

"I've seen three in a row, all alike. And the third man—one Baxter Cate, from Liberty Gun Works—implied that they weren't commercially available."

"Cate? What were you doing with him?"

"Turning down an offer to be his poster child. What do you know?"

"Only the rumor that his shop exists as a front so that he can stockpile weapons for the Inner Circle of Free Men, one of the sagebrush militias."

"The circle inside the star. But if they killed Charlie Castro, why draw attention to themselves by leaving the body tarred and feathered on the Sierra Express premises?"

"You're not really asking me that question."

"No."

"I don't think I'm up to speed on this. Why don't you go back to the beginning? Every painful detail of the past ten days."

I had barely started when Sandra interrupted.

"I don't remember anything about tar and feathers," she said.

"Matthews decided to hold that detail. And I shouldn't have mentioned it to you."

"I won't release it without an okay. But why tar and feathers on Castro's face?"

"In the nineteenth century, tar and feathers were used to mark undesirables. Whoever killed Charlie Castro wanted to make certain he was marked undesirable."

"Go on."

I went on, giving her every painful detail, and it took all of lunch and then some. At the beginning, she resisted the urge to take notes. By the end, she had apologized and taken out a pen and pad.

"You can't use this yet," I had warned.

"But I want to be ready," she'd replied.

We both reached for the check when I had finally wound down.

"I asked for a favor," I said.

"I'm expensing this," Sandra said. "And I'll hold the information until you tell me I can use it."

"There are two issues here, you know. One is that I don't want Matthews mad at me before I have something that'll make him forgive me at the same time. But the other is, I don't want you to do anything that's going to draw any more attention to me. I'm not going to be able to keep doing my job if I get too much attention. It's already a problem."

"I know. And we'll have to talk about that. Because you're going to get the attention, and you're going to have to choose whether it comes from me or from someone else."

"Okay." I took my hand off the check. "Another time."

I thought about the man in the bar. We would talk another time, my friend.

I thanked her for lunch, picked up the folder, and left. I walked down the escalator and hurried through the casino. I wanted to be home.

By the time I got there, I had worked my way back through the conversation to Sandra's advice on Curtis. Let him go, concentrate on what was before me. I hoped I could do it.

I settled down at my desk and opened the folder.

After reading the articles, I knew a bit more about Mike Danken, but nothing that could be called the full story on George Morales.

Shooting George Morales had given Danken the same fifteen minutes in the spotlight that shooting the younger

Morales had given me, the difference being that Danken was an off-duty cop. And he hadn't seen fit to moralize. He had mostly talked about law and order being a full-time job. I read the file twice, looking for a reference to Morales's wife and children, but there wasn't one. Morales was simply described as an unemployed construction worker, a resident of Sparks.

The second shooting wasn't much more complicated. Danken and his partner had been sent to check on a domestic violence complaint. The man had come running out of the house waving his gun as the two officers approached. Danken and his partner both drew their guns and warned the man to drop his. When he didn't, Danken shot.

Both times, the shootings were investigated, both times ruled justifiable. Even so, Danken chose to retire, take his pension, and become a mail-order minister. There was no hint that the retirement might have been requested, and I didn't think Matthews or anyone else would tell me if it had been.

Danken's former partner, Ralph Knox, was still a police officer, as far as I knew. I had only met him a couple of times, and he had struck me as one of those cowboy cops who practice quick draws in the mirror.

I was more interested in the description of the second victim. His name was Oscar Peralta, and he had lived in the same housing tract, off York Way, where the Castros and the Rashads lived, not far from the Zanzibar. I wondered if he had been a Chargers fan.

I was getting tired of the puzzle and I wanted a solution. Even if it meant threatening Robert Morales.

But that was a last resort. I read the articles one more time.

And I realized that someone else was missing from the

account besides Elva Morales: Louise Danken. I hadn't asked her any questions about the Morales family, because I hadn't known about the earlier connection.

I grabbed my sheepskin jacket and jogged the few blocks to the Danken house, raising an uncomfortable sweat. My sense of the residence as a church had slipped a little.

The office hours sign was still up, so I entered without knocking. The Christmas decorations were gone, and the mantel/altar looked bare without them.

I crossed to the archway.

"Louise?"

When she didn't answer, I started down the hall.

I found her in the kitchen, seated in the breakfast nook, staring into the backyard. She was wearing a faded pink bathrobe, no makeup, and her hair was limp and oily enough to have gone for a week without shampoo.

"Are you okay?" I asked.

"Probably not. But I could fix you a cup of tea."

A kettle was sitting on the stove. I filled it with water and turned on the electric burner.

"If you'll tell me where the cups are, I'll fix tea for both of us," I said.

She directed me to mugs and tea bags.

"Lemon Mist all right?" I asked.

When she didn't answer, I gave both of us Lemon Mist. I put the two mugs on the table and sat down.

"Tell me what you know," I said.

She gestured first toward the backyard.

"The snow so rarely stays on the ground. It really is beautiful."

"It is," I agreed. The peach curtains framed a white-on-white world. Bare outlines of tree and fence asserted themselves. A squirrel's track from one to the other was the only indication of life.

I took a sip of my tea and waited.

"Have you heard anything about Mike?" she asked.

"No. But I read some old articles from the *Herald*, including the one about the Morales shooting and the one about his retirement. Mike didn't tell me everything—he didn't come clean about his involvement in this. And if I'm going to keep looking for him, I need everything you know about the Morales family."

"They weren't a family," she replied.

"I don't understand. I thought George Morales was Jamie's father."

"Biologically, yes. But not in any of the ways that count. He never provided for his children, not food, not money, not affection. Elva kept finding jobs, mostly domestic or janitorial work, and George would occasionally find construction jobs, only to lose them again."

"Why?"

Louise shrugged. "Sometimes the job would end. Or he would get angry and hit somebody before the job ended. And then he was fired. Anyway, Elva finally threw him out. He was no help with the rent, no help with the boys—both little then—and she didn't want to pay for his food and clothes any longer. That was when he robbed the store and shot the clerk."

"And Mike shot him."

"Yes."

"When did Elva forgive Mike?"

"I don't know. He didn't try to talk with her until after he had retired. By then six years had passed, and she had decided that she really was better off without George. And when she realized the changes Mike had been through, Elva decided Mike might be able to do a better job than she could of getting through to Jamie. Jamie was already acting up, and Elva was worried about him."

"But Jamie wouldn't listen to Mike, any more than he would to Elva."

"No."

"When did Mike meet the Castros?"

"I don't remember. Both Jamie and Robert stayed with Elena when Elva was working. Charlie had a good job, so Elena didn't work at anything but the boys. Sometimes Mike would go over to the Castro house to find Jamie. He never really got to know Charlie."

"What about the Castro boys? What are they like?"

"Good boys—teenagers. Robert was closer to them in some ways than he was to his brother."

"I hope he'll stay that way." And I hoped I didn't have to use Robert as a threat. I had to change the subject. "Do you know anything about a group called the Inner Circle of Free Men?"

"What?"

I repeated the name.

"No." Louise shook her head slowly. "Who are they?"

"I don't know. They may not even be connected with this. What about Baxter Cate?"

"Baxter? What about him?"

"You know him?"

"I've met him." She wasn't thrilled with the admission. "He and Mike have some sort of financial deal, but I don't know what it is."

"And one more name. Oscar Peralta."

"Oh, God." She slumped over, hugging herself. "Oscar Peralta. The man who changed our lives."

"How?"

"Mike could argue—did argue—that George Morales was a bad man, a dangerous man who was the cause of his own destruction. He couldn't judge Oscar Peralta so easily."

"I thought Peralta was waving a gun."

"No." She looked up at me. When I saw what the admission was costing her, I almost asked her to stop. But I let her go on. "That was the official story. When Mike told me the truth—and it only came out because of his nightmares—I insisted that he take some kind of action. His action turned out to be resigning from the force. I hadn't really been asking for that, or I didn't think so at the time."

"The truth?" I prompted.

She picked up her mug and took a sip. I wasn't certain she was going to tell me. She put the mug down, turned toward the window, and said the words as softly as if she were talking to the tree.

"They—Mike and Ralph—Ralph Knox, Mike's partner—parked the black-and-white in front of the house, red lights flashing. Peralta came out of the house screaming, at them, at his wife, whatever. Ralph shot in the air. Mike heard the shot and fired. He hit Peralta, killed him. They planted the gun in Peralta's hand. I don't know which of them suggested it."

We both knew it didn't matter which one suggested it.

"But Peralta's wife must have known that he didn't have a gun," I said.

"She was tired and hurt and frightened, and at the time, she didn't think anyone would believe her."

"Later?"

"Later, Mike had retired from the force and become a minister. She came to him, angry. He convinced her that no good could come of a suddenly different story."

"Are you saying he told her it would be his word against hers?"

Louise didn't answer.

"What happened to her?" I asked.

"I don't know."

"Do you remember her first name? Anything that might help me trace her?"

"Why do you want to?" Her head jerked around, eyes alert, meeting mine.

"You asked me to find Mike. I still don't know what information is important and what isn't. If you remember her first name, I'd like to know what it is."

"Nita. Her first name was Nita."

"Nita? Just Nita? Or was it Anita? Juanita?"

"Just Nita, I think."

"Did anyone else know the truth about Oscar Peralta? Anyone who might have had a grudge against Mike?"

"Why do you think this is aimed at Mike?" she snapped. "Why are you investigating him instead of Charlie Castro? I thought all this was about finding who killed Charlie Castro."

"It is about that. But since there's a connection between Mike and Charlie, and Mike has disappeared, it's about Mike, too. You know that."

"I don't know that," she shook her head slowly. "If Nita Peralta wanted to hurt Mike, why would she wait?"

I waited until she was satisfied with her own answer, whatever it was.

"We should have left Reno," she continued. "I told him that. We should have sold the house and moved to Alaska. In Alaska, they would have been glad to see us. No one would have asked why he wanted to retire. Have you ever been to Alaska?"

"No."

"We went there once, on vacation. We should have moved there, I knew it."

"Is there anything else you can think of—anything remotely connected with Mike's retirement, or Oscar Peralta, or George Morales, or Charlie Castro, or anyone else, including Ralph Knox and Baxter Cate—that might help me find him?"

Louise shut her eyes and took a deep breath.

"No." The exhale was a long one.

"Okay. Call me if you think of anything."

"You're not quitting?" Her face was twisted, eyes meeting mine then glancing away, out the window again.

"No. Not right now, anyway. My promise was to Mike, not to you, and I'm not ready to quit."

The tears started again, the tears she didn't seem to notice, the same tears that had been so unnerving while she had been filling out the missing persons form.

"Thank you. Can I get you more tea?"

"No. No, thank you. I really need to get going on this. I'll stay in touch."

I was standing up and backing away as I said it. I took a slight nod as a good-bye.

I went straight out the front door without pausing. I wasn't certain that I had the full story on George Morales, but I had enough to make it worthwhile going back to see Baxter Cate, even though it meant driving downtown.

I had walked enough that day. I had to walk home to pick up the Jeep, but that would be enough.

The Mother Lode parking garage was close enough to the Liberty Gun Works. I cut through the casino and jaywalked across the street. Not even Piper Laurie and Tony Curtis could have slowed the traffic any more than the casino remodeling next door to the Mother Lode had. Car speed was practically down to gridlock, and I wasn't worried about being hit.

I needn't have hurried.

"Baxter didn't come in today," Morris informed me, smiling, after he had buzzed me in. "Too much New Year's cheer, I guess."

"You haven't heard from him?"

"No. But he keeps his own hours."

"Would you do me a favor? Give him a call at home and ask when I can see him."

"Of course." Morris picked up the phone and pressed the numbers. He handed me the receiver so that I could hear the machine answer.

I left my own message.

"Anything else?"

"Just let me out," I said.

I was relieved to hear the buzzer release the door lock. Even a few minutes in the cramped store with the smiling Morris had made me nervous.

I jaywalked back across Virginia, thinking what to do next. My only real choice at that point was whether to try to catch Letty Rashad when she got off work, hoping her mother had talked to her, or to go home. Much as I wanted to go home, I drove to Sierra Express.

The red Toyota wasn't parked in front of the building.

I might have cruised around a little, or at least tried to check out the part of the lot in back of the building, but no sooner had I slowed down than a big blue-and-white truck zoomed around the corner of Fourth onto Valley Road and was suddenly inches from the tail of the Jeep. I stepped on the gas to get out of its way. The momentum carried me all the way to the next corner, where I paused to check traffic.

Glancing back, I noticed that the truck had parked in such a way that the entrance to the lot was partially blocked. This didn't seem the best moment to approach the place, so I headed back toward home.

I had reached Mill and High, and I was about to turn into my own driveway when I realized that someone else had parked there first. A gold Mercedes sedan was sitting next to my house.

I drove straight past and parked in the next block. I

approached the Mercedes cautiously, keeping to the shadows as much as possible. No one was in it.

And no one had walked from the Mercedes to my front door. The covering of snow was marked by the tracks my boots had left in the morning, but only a bird or a child with small feet and a large stride could have gone the other way.

Sundance trotted around the corner of the house and started digging in the relatively protected, but still frozen, dirt under the lilac bush. As he arched his back to relieve himself, I felt guilty for expecting the cats to share a dirty litter box. On the plus side, he wasn't nervous. If anybody but Ramona had been snooping around, he would have been nervous. And this wasn't Ramona's car. So no one was hiding out, waiting for me.

I walked around the Mercedes, inspecting it.

I wouldn't have forced the Mercedes trunk, even if I had found dark red spots on the bumper. But someone had thoughtfully left the lid ajar. I slipped my hand under the edge and flipped it up.

I was braced to find a body. Specifically, I was braced to find Mike Danken's body.

But the dead eyes staring somewhere past me weren't Mike's. The tarred and feathered face belonged to Baxter Cate.

Chapter 16

"WHAT HAVEN'T YOU told me?" Matthews asked.

At least he didn't sound angry. Resigned, annoyed, but not angry.

Matthews and Michelle Urrutia hadn't taken more than ten minutes to travel the two blocks from the police station. We had talked logistics—when I had gotten home, how I had found the car, why I had flipped the trunk lid—until the rest of the crime scene crew arrived. Then I had invited Matthews into my office and offered him one of the black and white cowhide client chairs. I took my own seat behind the desk. The sad eyes and heavy jowls were intimidating, and I needed all the help I could get.

"I promised Mike I'd back him up. So I was asking a few questions. And you might have told me that he shot George Morales, Jamie's father. I really deserved to have that information." Sometimes the best defense is an offense.

But life isn't football.

"Maybe you did," Matthews answered. "I don't know. I wouldn't have thought it was my place to tell you what Mike did years ago. Mike could tell you if he wanted to.

And it was a matter of public record—all you had to do was look it up. So you have that information. What I did tell you was to stay out of an ongoing police investigation, which you didn't do. So tell me what you did to deserve a body in your driveway."

"I wish I knew."

He shifted in the chair, resting his chin in one meaty hand, dangling the other on his knee. He looked ready to wait forever, so I told him the story of the past few days.

"I think this has to be tied to Sierra Express," I ended, "but I don't know why anybody there would draw attention to the place by leaving a body in the back parking lot."

Matthews raised his eyebrows. When he didn't say anything, I didn't add my own thought, the one that had finally hit me. Which was, maybe whoever it was hadn't intended to leave the body there long. If I had messed up somebody's plan, somebody had paid me back by dumping Baxter Cate's body on me. Baxter Cate, who had suggested I might want to leave town for a while.

Michelle Urrutia broke the silence by opening my front door and walking in as if she belonged in my office. I hadn't locked the door. I was still annoyed. She should have knocked.

"Were you expecting a delivery from Sierra Express this afternoon?" she asked.

I don't know what my face looked like, but she frowned and rushed to the desk.

"Are you okay?" She placed a hand on my shoulder. "If you put your head between your knees, the blood will come back."

"I'm not going to faint." I brushed her hand away. "And no, I wasn't expecting a delivery. What made you ask?"

"Well, I knocked on a couple of doors, to see if any of your neighbors had noticed the driver of the Mercedes, and nobody had. But the woman who lives across the street did notice a Sierra Express truck. She bought a new television set at an after-Christmas sale, and she's been waiting for days for the delivery. She saw the truck parked in front of your house, that was all." Michelle was still frowning. She backed away a step or two, staying close enough that she could catch me if I fell over.

I closed my eyes long enough to clear my vision. When I opened them, Matthews was still watching me.

"I'd hate to imagine what your face would look like," he said, "after the tar and feathers."

"Don't."

"I'm not trying to scare you. I just want you to think before you act."

"About the tar and feathers. You kept that quiet last time. Are you keeping it quiet again?"

"Probably."

"Have you kept it quiet before?"

Matthews thought before answering.

"You probably do deserve that information. Three times before in the last five years. All Hispanic."

"Then you're looking for a serial killer. Shouldn't the press know that?"

"Not my decision. And we haven't been certain it was the same perp each time. Small differences, but enough. Besides, Cate isn't Hispanic."

I let that sink in.

"What do you plan on doing?" I asked.

"Wrapping up the crime scene and going home," he said. "In the morning, I'll see about getting a warrant to search the Sierra Express building and grounds."

"What you're saying is, Kovanda isn't going to run."

"I don't even know that Kovanda is involved in this, and neither do you. Maybe you made a bad impression, so he didn't want to talk to you. He was polite every time I saw him, and I expect him to be polite tomorrow."

"And he's had time to get anything off the premises that he wants to get off the premises."

Matthews nodded. "He's had almost two weeks to do that. Another night won't matter."

"Don't you ever wish you could move without a warrant?"

"All the time. No, that's not right." He took his chin off his hand and leaned forward. "Let me put it this way. I wish I could call a judge and make it happen right now. I wish I had some way of making sure Kovanda would tell me the truth when I talk to him, whether he wants to or not. I wish I had some way of making trials be about truth and justice, not about lawyer skills. That's three wishes, and I don't have a magic lamp with a genie to make them come true. So they're wishes, and that's all. I'm a cop. I've been one for a long time. That's all I want to be. So I play by the rules. More than that, I live by the rules."

"Hell, Matthews, you even believe in the rules," I said.

He barely nodded. "Promise me you won't go out tonight, O'Neal."

"I haven't had dinner."

"I'll call for a pizza. I'll even pay for the pizza." He clasped his hands, entreating.

"What makes you think I'd keep the promise?"

"That question does. If you were going to lie to me, you would have done it without hedging."

"If I promise that, will you promise to call me tomorrow and tell me what's going on at Sierra Express?"

"I will."

"Done. And you don't have to pay for the pizza."

We stood up and shook hands on it. I was tired, and I meant to keep the promise. I really wasn't lying.

While I was standing, I shook hands with Michelle, too. She still looked ready to catch me if I fainted, even though she was maybe four inches shorter and ten pounds lighter than I was.

I walked outside with them. Everything was gone—the photographer, the ambulance, the Mercedes—except the car that would take them back to the police station.

My Jeep was still on the street. I didn't feel like moving it.

I watched them drive away and went back inside.

This time, I locked the door.

I sat down at my desk and put my head between my knees. Not that I was going to faint. I just needed a little better blood circulation.

The day was gone. I had promised to stay in until the next. And Matthews was right. I had to think before I acted. Whenever I acted.

I was quietly contemplating the meaning of action when the phone rang.

"If you're serious about finding Charlie Castro's killers, then I'm willing to talk to you."

The voice was vaguely familiar.

"I'm serious. And I'd like to know who I'd be talking with."

"I'll tell you when I see you, my friend. If you are my friend."

The man from the Zanzibar, the one who had been sitting across from the guy in bifocals.

"Fine. I'll meet you tomorrow. You name the time and place."

"Tonight."

"Not tonight. I've had a bad day."

"Tonight, if you're serious. Tomorrow may be too late."

I struggled with the conflict between my promise to Mike

Danken—and, by some kind of transference, Louise—in the Castro case and my promise to Matthews to stay out of it for this one night.

"When and where?" I was feeling damned if I did, damned if I didn't, and if there is a God, I hoped she understood.

"Nine o'clock. The Wreck Room. You know it? On Commercial Way?"

"I've been by. I can find it."

The phone clicked in my ear as he hung up.

The Wreck Room looked like a particularly sleazy bar, in a sleazy neighborhood, and not a meeting place I would have chosen. But I was stuck with it.

I had about two hours in which to eat something, and I really needed to eat something.

I checked the refrigerator out of some atavistic habit, knowing it was virtually empty. I opened a beer and fed the cats.

When the doorbell rang, I was standing in the hall, beer can in hand, on my way back to my office.

"Who is it?" I shouted, edging toward the bedroom.

I wasn't expecting anyone, and one gun was on the dresser, the other in it.

"Pizza delivery," a voice called. "Already paid for."

"Leave it on the porch."

I traded the beer can for the All American and proceeded to the door. Sounds indicated something being placed, someone walking away.

I opened the door a crack. An innocent pizza box sat on the mat, oozing grease and reeking of pepperoni.

I slipped the gun into my boot and brought the pizza box to my desk. If I hadn't been so hungry, I would have felt too guilty to eat.

Matthews had sprung for a large. He must have figured I might need breakfast, too.

At about quarter to nine I left for the Wreck Room, the pizza still churning in my stomach.

My anonymous caller had picked a bar that was little more than a shed crammed between a salvage yard and an auto body shop. There was a dim neon sign over the door, and dim lights at the entrance to the small parking lot, as if somebody wanted to save on electricity.

I wanted to make certain I could get out in a hurry if necessary, so I parked the Jeep on the street. The lack of streetlights left me none too comfortable about that, either.

I checked the parking lot as I crossed. There were only two cars, and neither looked familiar.

The inside of the bar was as dimly lit as the outside. I might have had trouble picking out my man, but he and the bartender were the only people in the place.

The bartender pulled two draft beers without speaking, and my self-styled friend carried them to a small table.

"John Gonzales," he said.

I nodded and sat. "Thanks for the beer, John."

John Gonzales was wearing a brown work shirt and jeans. He had left a patterned wool jacket lying on the bar. I couldn't distinguish much more about him.

"Tell me your involvement in this," he said.

His face seemed blurred, whether because the light was dim or I was tired. I knew his eyes were dark, that was about all.

I told him about finding Castro, about Danken's disappearance, even about Cate. I didn't see a reason to lie. Except about my promise to Matthews, to stay in that night. I left that out.

"Your turn," I said.

"I don't understand about Cate." He shook his head. "I thought I understood what happened to Charlie, but I don't understand why they would kill Cate."

"Who?"

He shook his head again. "Maybe the Inner Circle of Free Men want nothing more than death for everyone but themselves. Cate was white, like them. Why would they kill him?"

I hadn't mentioned the belt buckles. I wondered if Cate had been wearing his when he died.

"I have no idea," I said. "What made you mention that group?"

"Because of Charlie. Charlie had some wild conspiracy story that he told me, about the Inner Circle of Free Men, and how they were going to destroy him."

"Is that what Charlie Castro was doing on Tuesday and Thursday nights? Trying to get something on the Inner Circle?"

"Yes. He was following someone, every Tuesday and Thursday, to a meeting, then following some other member home. He wanted to find out who all of them were, from where they lived."

"What did Charlie tell you about the Inner Circle?" I took a sip of the beer. It was cold and malty, and I began to pick up a little.

"That they are a group of white men who believe they have been chosen by God to live, to survive the turmoil that is coming at the turn of the century. Because they are chosen, whatever they do is right. And part of what they want to do is to make certain that no one of what they call mixed blood joins them in their New World."

"What is mixed blood?"

John shrugged. "Certainly those of us with brown skins and Spanish surnames qualify. Mestizos."

Either the beer was taking effect, or I was getting used to the dim light. His features took shape. Whatever Spanish conqueror had given John his name had finally lost to the Aztec who had given him his face.

"Shit. Anybody whose ancestors have been in this country—and especially the West—long enough probably qualifies. Half the Daughters of the American Revolution probably qualify under those rules, if it comes to that, if you think about the percentage of the people on this continent in 1776 who were of either African or native American descent."

"Tell them."

"Who are they? Do you have any names?"

"Charlie didn't say any, not even the name of the one he followed. He only said what he overheard when he followed the man to the meetings. He said that these men have decided that they are no longer subject to the laws of this country. They want to move to the desert and form a new community, although they argue over where it is to be. They want to call it Israel."

"Do you know where they meet?"

"No. But we can find out."

"How?"

John leaned forward, almost overbalancing the small table. He had to grab his beer. "There must be a record of the meeting place in the Sierra Express office, because that is where Charlie first found out about the group. And no one will be in the office tonight. They will all be at the meeting."

"Come on. You can't be suggesting we break in."

"Why not?"

"Because it would be illegal, and we won't gain more than a few hours anyway. Matthews is getting a warrant in the morning. The police will be there by afternoon."

"Will they know what they're looking for?"

"Do you?"

"Better than some rookie cop."

"No. I won't do it. Matthews isn't a rookie, and he knows the Inner Circle may have something to do with the murders. This isn't a good idea."

"You see, gringa, you don't really want to help. You only want to talk."

"That's not fair."

"You're going to tell me that some of your best friends are Mexican, right?"

"Come on. Are you still beating your wife?"

He chuckled. "Okay. Does that mean you're coming?"

"No."

"Then I'm going alone."

"Why? Why is this so urgent?"

"Because people are disappearing and dying around you, and I'm talking to you. If I don't move, do something, I may be next."

He tossed down the rest of his beer and pushed the chair back. I watched him pick up his jacket from the bar, put it on, and head toward the door.

"Okay," I said. "I'll come."

I had already broken my promise to Matthews. And I knew I couldn't live with myself if I let John Gonzales go to Sierra Express alone and then stumbled across his body in the morning. I followed him out into the lot.

"My car," I said.

"Both cars. I'll park a block or so away from the lot and meet you at the entrance."

I wasn't going to ride with him, and if he didn't want to ride with me, he was right—it would have to be both cars, although two cars made it twice as likely that someone would notice us.

"Meet you there," I said.

He drove off in a dark blue Chevrolet that sounded as if

a Harley mechanic had given it a tune-up. Another reason to take my own car. I hoped he parked three blocks away.

I decided to park the Jeep on Elko Avenue and see if I could come at the lot from the back. As long as there were no dogs. This was the kind of area where any late-night guards would be canine. I hadn't seen any at Sierra Express, but I didn't know what the neighbors might have.

I tried to think back to the night I had found Charlie Castro in the trunk of his Honda. What had been on the other side of the chain link fence? In my memory, something heavy and hulking was there. I couldn't manage to fine-tune the image.

The address belonged to a nursery, the kind with a big sign that said WHOLESALE TO THE PUBLIC. I cheered up a little. Nobody would worry about plants being stolen, especially in January.

I parked the Jeep, grabbed my flashlight, and walked up to the locked gate.

"Yo, dog," I whispered, just in case I was wrong.

Nothing answered.

"Yo, dog," I said a little louder.

A sharp bark jerked me around.

A Rottweiler was regarding me from across the street, behind another chain link fence, assessing how likely I was to invade the lumberyard he considered his territory.

"Stay," I said with what I hoped was much authority.

He stayed. Right where he was. But at least he didn't bark again, not even when I began to climb the nursery fence. Chain link fences provide easy toeholds for boots.

I was on the other side and away from the gate before I took a deep breath. The dog was still quiet.

I flicked on the flashlight and checked the area ahead of me, then flicked it off and shut my eyes, focusing on the image that remained on my retina. A short parking lot, then a path that led past a building into what looked like an arctic jungle. I opened my eyes, letting them readjust to the scene. I crossed the lot and found the path. Then I turned on the flashlight again, keeping the beam pointed low to the ground.

The jungle was mostly potted junipers frosted with the last of the snow. I moved cautiously down the aisle between the plants. When something brushed my leg, I jerked into a leftover Douglas fir, unsold at Christmas.

"Meow," the something said.

Nurseries may not have a problem with thefts, but they do with rodents.

"Meow to you, too," I whispered.

I reached down and gave the cat a friendly pat. She finished leaving her scent on my jeans and disappeared. The aisle led straight to the back fence. The image of something heavy and hulking resolved itself into stacks of terra-cotta pots.

I jammed the flashlight into my waistband and scaled the chain link barrier.

Only when I was on the other side, checking the dark row of Sierra Express trucks for movement, did I admit to myself how much I had wanted to do this. With or without John Gonzales, I wanted to know what was in the Sierra Express files.

And I didn't want to wait for Matthews and his warrant.

I slid over to the shadow of the trucks and moved along until I could see the front of the building.

"Ssssss."

I froze.

"I see you by the truck. Come on."

A figure stepped briefly away from the glass doors and then back again. If John hadn't moved, I wouldn't have spotted him.

The bright space between the truck and the building was narrow, lit from a pole near the street. I crossed to the next shadow as quickly as I could.

"How difficult is the door lock?" I whispered.

"The hell with the lock," he answered.

I heard the glass smash once, then again. He reached through and unlocked the door.

"Shit. I thought this was going to be subtle."

He didn't answer.

"What are you holding?" I asked. No fear. I wasn't afraid of this man. And if I felt a little anxiety, I had to keep it out of my voice.

"A jack. I needed something heavy."

He pushed the door open, and I followed him through.

I turned on the flashlight. The office looked much as it had the last time I had been there, just the file cabinets against the wall and a mess of papers on the desk next to the computer.

"You want the files or the desk?" I asked.

"I want the computer," he answered. "And keep that beam pointed toward the floor."

I started to bristle, but he was right. In the dim glow, I watched him sit down at the desk and boot up the computer.

"Lousy, stripped-down PC clone," he muttered. "Not so much as a modem. No way to get to its files except by checking its directory on site."

"Oh, hell. What do you know that you didn't tell me in the bar?"

"Nothing."

"Come on. Was Charlie Castro your brother-in-law or what?"

"No."

He was scrolling through the directory as if he knew what he was looking for. He hit the Escape key, typed a couple of commands, and a list of names and addresses appeared on the screen.

"Shine your light on the printer," he said.

I did so briefly. He flipped the switch, hit a few more keys on the computer, and the list began to print.

"Why was Charlie following people instead of just stealing the list?" I asked.

"This was the only way to steal the list. Someone had to be desperate enough to break in." He typed another series of commands, brought up another file, scanned it, then escaped from it.

"What did you need me for?"

"An alibi. Which you must give me because you are the obvious suspect. We will take the list back to the Wreck Room, phone an anonymous prowler tip to the police, wait until we are certain they have responded. The bartender will say we were there for hours." Gonzales had been watching as two pages slipped past the roller. He picked them up and glanced at me, smiling for the first time. "The bartender is my brother-in-law."

"Fingerprints?"

"Off a dirty keyboard?" He shook his head and turned back to the printer. Something else, not the list of names, was coming through. "Not even in the movies. And I didn't touch anything else. Did you?"

"No. Let's go."

"Where?"

The word was said so softly that I almost didn't hear it above the low hum of the printer and the slightly higher whirr of the PC fan. But I did hear it, and I knew Gonzales hadn't said it.

I started to turn my head, very slowly and carefully.

A heavy hand landed on my left shoulder, and something

round and hard like a gun barrel was jammed into the base of my spine.

"Oh, shit." I dropped my flashlight. The beam spun around the room and went out.

Gonzales jerked away from the printer. His eyes found the face over my shoulder.

"Don't do this," he said.

"You first," the voice said. "Out the door."

Gonzales nodded. Without shifting his focus, he got up and moved toward the door. With the hand and the gun barrel pressing me on, I followed.

Gonzales pushed through the door and stopped outside, looking again at the face over my shoulder.

"Don't do this, my friend. Please."

"Truck number three is unlocked. Open the back and climb in," the voice ordered.

Gonzales nodded and crossed to the truck.

The big man—all I knew about him—was so close on my heels that I was practically tripping over my own feet to keep ahead of him.

Gonzales opened the back doors and turned again.

"Go on," the voice said.

Gonzales started to say something. At least, he opened his mouth.

The man moved the gun away from the small of my back.

I felt his arm come above my shoulder and heard the ping of the silencer. Gonzales's head jerked backward. His body slumped partly into the truck, then crumpled to the asphalt.

Under normal circumstances, I wouldn't attack a man who had a gun. But I figured I was dead either way, and I'd rather go fighting. I brought my left elbow up and jammed it hard into the soft tissue just below his sternum. With my right hand I grabbed for the gun.

And I almost got it. But his right hand came back with mine, then up. The gun barrel crashed into my temple.

I tried to hold on to consciousness, but I couldn't stand upright. Before I hit the ground, I was lifted into the air and tossed into the truck. I was listening for the ping of the silencer when I blacked out.

Chapter
17

AT FIRST, I was afraid I was blind. My right temple was throbbing and I couldn't see. I had flickered in and out of awareness a couple of times before I opened my eyes, and then I was sorry I hadn't kept them shut.

The truck was in motion, I knew that. The ride was smooth—we had to be on one of the interstates.

I struggled to sit up, closing my eyes to deal with the internal havoc. When I opened them again, I caught a glimmer of light from a window in the partition that separated the back from the cab. Not enough to see anything. I crawled closer to the window.

My hand hit cloth-covered flesh. An arm.

If it was John Gonzales's arm, I didn't want to touch his head. And I couldn't crawl over his body.

I took the long way around.

As I neared the window, I began to see shapes. The windshield, the front of the truck beyond the cab. I caught a glimpse of an Exit sign. We were on Interstate 80, passing the university, heading west.

The driver was looking straight ahead.

I reached down and checked my boot. My gun wasn't there. I wondered if it had fallen out when I was tossed into the truck. I felt along the floor, back in the direction I had crawled from.

The truck glided right, up an exit ramp. A sudden stop threw me against Gonzales's body.

I dragged myself forward in time to catch the driver's profile in the glow from the streetlight as he checked the traffic before turning right.

A heavy, round cheek, and bifocals. The man from the Zanzibar. Gonzales's friend indeed.

The truck moved again, completing the right turn.

I caught the lights from a minimall before we moved into a darker residential district. I tried to find a street sign, but either my mind or my eyes couldn't quite focus.

The driver turned left. Uphill. The streetlights were gone so quickly that we must have been on McCarran Boulevard, at the edge of the city.

I had to shut my eyes again, trying to ease my throbbing temple. I opened them again when the truck slowed, then turned, then stopped.

When I looked out the window, the world was evenly black.

The door to the cab opened and slammed shut.

I sat in the quiet, in the dark, huddled away from John Gonzales's body, for some undetermined period of time. Then I heard voices, too low to make out the words.

I crawled toward the doors.

"Miss O'Neal?" someone called. "If you can hear me, move away from the doors. We're going to open them, and we don't want any sudden moves. We don't plan to hurt you, not if you cooperate."

I moved back, just short of the body.

The doors clicked, then opened.

I still couldn't see very much.

Rough hands helped me down from the truck. Not the driver. Another man, one I didn't recognize. Two more men, one of them the driver—the shooter—stood by.

"This way," the man who had helped me said, pointing toward a nearby house. A porch light with heavy wattage gave some illumination to the area.

The truck sat nose in toward a hillside. Between the truck and the house about half a dozen cars were parked haphazardly in the dirt that passed for a front yard.

The house itself was long and low. For two or three feet above the foundation, it was covered in old brick. Above that, redwood. Somebody had big plans for this house.

The man kept his hand on my elbow, guiding me toward the front door. I thought about jerking away, but I decided to save any sudden moves until one might do me some good.

The door had been left open. The man led me through a living room, lit only by one dim table lamp, to a hall. Another open door showed a well-lit flight of stairs leading down.

I glanced at the man, hoping his face would register. He might have been one of the group in the Zanzibar, but I wasn't certain.

He gestured toward the stairs, and I started down.

Waiting at the bottom of the stairs was Mike Danken.

"Freddie! Are you all right? The right side of your face is swollen! Let me look at it."

I stood stiffly while he examined my right temple.

"Get her some ice for this, will you? Please." That was said over my shoulder.

I heard the man move back up the stairs.

"I thought you were missing, Mike."

"I am, in a way. Out of sight to think things through." His brown eyes were clear and untroubled. He looked rested.

"There have been some pretty anxious people. Louise is one of them." I kept my voice level. No sudden moves.

"I'm sorry about that, and I'll explain it to her when I'm ready. She'll understand—she's my wife."

"What have you been thinking?"

I heard the man coming back. Mike reached past me to grasp a kitchen towel wrapped around some ice cubes.

"Thanks, Jack."

The man mumbled something in response.

Mike pressed the towel against my temple. I jerked away, then recovered.

"Sorry," Mike said.

"It's okay. The cold startled me." I took the makeshift pack, rearranged it, and held it gently over the swollen area.

"Come on in and meet the others. I'm actually glad you're here. We've had some disagreements over how to handle this."

"Handle what?"

"Well, you." The eyes were still clear as he looked at me. "Come on."

The room at the foot of the stairs, the one in which we were standing, seemed to be nothing more than a storage area taking up about half the space of the floor above it. There were shelves on two of the walls, cartons stacked against a third. The fourth appeared to be solid concrete.

The door through the concrete was under the stairs.

I coughed when I entered. Several people had evidently been smoking, and the ventilation wasn't good. The icy towel cleared my nose. I put it back on my forehead, hoping

I looked hurt. I was hurt. But maybe not as badly as they expected me to be.

The room was furnished as if it were a hunting lodge — the walls were crowded with mounted trophies, mostly deer heads, and two wild boars. A dozen leather chairs were arranged in a horseshoe, facing the entrance. Ten of them were occupied. Mike sat in one of the two empties, at the edge nearest me. Nobody seemed to be more central than anyone else.

I recognized Joe Kovanda and Ralph Knox, Mike's former partner. None of the others. All except Mike Danken were wearing the same belt buckle, the gold circle within the star.

I wished I could have been cheered, recognizing Ralph, a cop, in the group. But the expression on his face let me know that he wasn't going to help me.

"I'm sorry we don't have a chair for you," Mike said.

I didn't point out the vacancy.

"Nobody will mind if you sit on the floor," he added.

The floor was concrete, with a drain in the center.

"I'll stand," I said. I hoped I could. I could if they didn't talk for too long.

The man Mike had called Jack was standing beside the door. If he could stand, I could.

Jack moved aside. Two men—the shooter and the other one from the parking area—came in. They dumped John Gonzales next to me. When the other man stood, I recognized the smashed cheek. I had seen him with Joe Kovanda at Sierra Express.

"He's still alive," the shooter said.

I winced. I should have checked, in the truck. I had been so certain Gonzales was dead that I hadn't felt for a pulse. Not that it would have helped.

"Good," Joe Kovanda said. "That helps."

"Helps what?" I asked. "Are you going to help him?"

"No."

I wanted to be glad something helped, but he wasn't looking at me, and the tone in his voice wasn't reassuring.

The shooter and the smashed cheek moved to the wall beside Jack, all three near the door.

I edged toward the wall on the other side of the door.

Leaning might be a good idea.

Gonzales wasn't moving. I was going to have to take the shooter's word for it that Gonzales was still alive.

"I'm probably the one who should explain the situation," Mike Danken said.

"Okay," I answered. "I'd like to hear about it."

"This group—the Inner Circle of Free Men—has a legacy of independence from any governmental body that comes straight from the earliest days of this territory."

"Nevada is a State," I interrupted. "You have a legacy from the men who voted to join the Union."

"And I'm certain they had their reasons," he replied. "Although there were arguments, even at the time, as I'm sure you know, about how much authority they wanted to give away. Many didn't feel they were ceding much—after all, the Tenth Amendment to the Constitution, the last of the Bill of Rights, reserves to the States all powers not specifically granted to the federal government. Once the War Between the States ended, and it became clear that only ordinary citizens could maintain law and order out here, there were other disagreements about government."

"If all this turns out to be about the Second Amendment, you can let me go now. I believe in the right to bear arms." Except for kids, I thought. And maybe assault weapons ought to be regulated. The man with the bifocals standing next to Jack had a license to drive. He didn't have a license to shoot.

"Well, it's about a little more than that," Danken said.

"Okay. Which amendment gives you the right to shoot people, and tar and feather them, because of the color of their skin?" I was too tired to argue history.

"Nobody has to give us any rights," Kovanda said. "We're born with all the rights we need. Including the right to set up our own government, with our own laws, and to decide who lives in our territory. All the government we've got now does is take rights, in exchange for nothing."

"If you have the right to kill anybody you want to kill, if everybody has that right, then we can't call ourselves a civilization," I said.

Danken nodded, smiling as if he were pleased with me. "That's why we've been talking about moving outside the city and starting over."

"Easier than shooting half the population and trying to claim whatever's left," I said.

"Get to the point, Mike," Kovanda said. "Don't argue with her."

"If the point is some kind of racial purity, what happens to your son's girlfriend?" I asked.

"We let her alone as long as he likes her. But I've told him, no children with a breed. And that isn't the point I meant," Kovanda answered. He stirred in his chair and glared at Danken.

"We need to know where you stand," Danken said. "That's the point. There's been some confusion."

"I would have said that about you," I replied.

"I can understand why you might feel that way." Danken nodded, still smiling.

I was beginning to get the same feeling about Danken that

I had about the smiling guy in the gun store. Something wasn't quite right about that smile.

"When did you join these guys?" I asked.

Danken hesitated, frowning, as if he had to decide which of us was going to answer questions first.

"I was asked to join several times over the years," he said. "And I thought about it carefully. I came to the conclusion that they were right and I belonged with them on the day I disappeared from my old life."

"So this whole thing was a fraud? You knew your buddies were responsible for Charlie Castro's murder all along?" I was glad I was holding the ice. A surge of anger sent blood to my head, and the ice drained away the heat of it.

"No. There are clear lines between members and outsiders—that's why the group is called the Inner Circle. I knew about the plans for a new community, a pure community, but I didn't know about the actions that had been taken to help purge Reno of undesirables."

"By that you mean the serial killings, the dead men marked with tar and feathers, the way Charlie Castro was."

Danken nodded. "It made sense, once Ralph told me. He tried to tell me years ago, after an incident with an undesirable named Peralta, but I didn't listen. I wanted to take my own path. Actually, I realized Ralph was right because of you. After all my work with the Morales boy, he turned out to be just like his father. An undesirable. Did you know I shot George Morales when he was robbing a store?"

"Yes. I heard that."

"And I thought I might have made a mistake, so I tried to make up for it by saving the son. But I couldn't do it. Ralph had told me several times over the years that I was wasting my energy, that I should shoot the boy and be done with it, but I didn't want to believe him." Danken glanced over at Ralph Knox, who sat stony and unmoving. "Even when you shot Jamie Morales for me, I didn't realize, not at first. Once Charlie was found dead, though, and I followed the trail here, Ralph and Joe and the others made it clear to me, finally, that it was us against them, all of them. Because if we didn't destroy them, they would destroy us. That was when I decided to join my true friends."

I wanted to tell him that I hadn't shot Jamie Morales for him, that I hadn't shot Jamie for anyone but Curtis. But I didn't want to mention Curtis in that room.

"Why didn't you just go home at that point? Louise would have stopped worrying, Matthews would have stopped worrying, and God only knows—" I only hesitated for an instant, and Danken didn't blink—"if Matthews could have traced the murders here."

"Would you have dropped the case?"

"I don't know."

"This way, you have no choice. And you and I can go in tomorrow to see Roy, with an explanation that will take him in another direction. I was kidnapped. You saved me. He'll have no choice to accept whatever we tell him."

"Maybe. But you're sure doing a lot—and expecting me to do a lot—for friends who turn and destroy their friends," I said.

"If you're referring to Baxter Cate, that was a copycat killing. The man on the floor shot Baxter, to make it look as if we were turning on our own." Danken gestured toward Gonzales. "A former Sierra Express employee. Joe underestimated him, as he underestimated Castro."

I glanced at Joe Kovanda. He didn't react.

"We were planning to make Gonzales our next example," Danken continued. "And now you can help."

Knox picked up a gun from the floor beside his chair, got up, and walked toward me. He ejected the clip and slipped it into his pocket.

"There's one bullet in the chamber," he said, holding the gun out. "Shoot him."

I was still holding the ice against my head. I didn't reach for the gun.

"What happens if I don't?" I asked.

"Then I have to shoot you," Danken said. He must have had a gun beside his chair, too, because one had appeared in his hand. "You decide. Literally a life and death decision. Gonzales dies either way. But if you shoot him, you live."

I wondered how many guns were in the room. Placing your gun beside your chair would be a way of showing you were here in peace, like checking it at the entrance to the saloon or in the sheriff's office had been. I suspected there was a lot of artillery on the floor. And whatever choice I made, I wasn't likely to leave the room alive.

The door was still open, but the three men were still leaning against the wall next to it. If I turned the gun on them, I'd just be shot in the back.

I had to decide how I wanted to die.

That was all.

When I realized I had no other choice, I felt something snap inside my chest. My whole body began to cool, as if my heart had stopped sending blood through my veins. My hands were the temperature of the ice. I placed the towel on the floor, stepped forward, and reached for the gun.

"Good-bye, John," I said, looking down at Gonzales.

I raised the gun, turned, and shot Danken between the eyes.

On the slim chance that everyone was off guard, I dropped to a crouch and dove for the doorway.

I landed against two pairs of boots.

"Nobody move. You're all under arrest."

Two officers in full battle gear stepped over me into the room. I crawled past them, out the door.

Matthews was standing at the foot of the stairs.

"The cavalry's here, O'Neal," he said. "You can get up now. You're saved."

I wanted to tell him better late than never, but the words stuck in my throat.

Chapter 18

IF RALPH KNOX hadn't confirmed that I was being held against my will, I might have had to spend what remained of the night in jail. Matthews seemed to believe that Knox would tell the truth about the rest of it, too.

He was right about that, at least.

"Knox understood that leading a double life could come back to haunt him," Matthews said when we talked the next day. "He's known that ever since he planted the gun on Peralta."

"You knew about that?"

"Yeah, but I couldn't prove it. And I could have been wrong." He smiled, pleased that he hadn't been. "When Danken became a minister, I thought maybe he had planted the gun. But Knox admitted it—waived his Miranda rights, on tape, and talked. So you're a hero again, O'Neal. This will go to a grand jury, but you'll come out of it all right. I won't even beat you up for breaking your promise to stay home."

"I've beat myself up enough about that. And I don't owe you for the pizza."

Matthews shrugged. "Come on. I had to get somebody close enough to drop a homing beeper in your Jeep, just in case you felt compelled to break that promise. I wasn't certain enough to post somebody. Now I wish I had. And you didn't help by parking where you did. By the time our guy responded to the beep, got to Elko Avenue, and figured out he was behind Sierra Express, you were in the truck. We were playing catch-up all night."

"Until the end."

"Yeah. You sleep okay?"

"Yeah." I lied. "I was exhausted." That was the truth.

"Talk to somebody. I'm sorry I was wrong about Danken." His jowls sagged as he said it. "But talk to somebody."

"Sure." I nodded. I'd have to think about that.

"I'll let you know if your gun turns up."

"Thanks."

The All American that had been in my boot hadn't surfaced in the search, although the cartons in the storage area of the cellar had been filled with enough guns and ammunition to hold out for a lengthy siege. Knox told Matthews that Cate had been stockpiling them there for months.

"Anything more?" I asked.

"I guess you don't care, but Gonzales is going to make it. The bullet smashed his cheekbone and pretty much took his ear off, but it didn't hit his brain."

"He really did kill Cate?"

"So Knox said. The group was keeping an eye on Gonzales. And Knox has no reason to lie about that."

"Then no, I don't think I care."

"Talk to somebody, O'Neal. Promise."

"Okay."

"And keep it this time."

I said good-bye and left the station.

When I had left the night before, I had had the company of a police officer who had driven me home and offered to stay until I could call a friend or my mother or anyone else I wanted.

I had thanked him for the offer and sent him away.

I had shivered under the blankets all night long, shaking so badly that both cats had retreated to far corners of the bed.

This day I was still cold, but the shivering had stopped.

And I had to talk to Curtis at least, whether I wanted to or not.

He was sitting up, reading a newspaper, when I entered the room. Tola Rae wasn't there.

He looked at me and frowned.

"You may need this bed when I get out of it," he said. "What happened?"

"A bad night last night. Where's Tola Rae?"

"At my apartment. Packing."

"For both of you." It wasn't a question.

Curtis nodded. "She's made some kind of special flight arrangements. We're leaving tomorrow. I'm only going for a few weeks." He added that too quickly. "Just until I'm strong enough to take care of myself again. Are you sure you don't want to talk about your bad night?"

I studied him for a moment, not sure whether I wanted to talk. The tubes were gone, and he seemed pretty much to be his old self, except for the lack of color in his face and the lack of energy in his eyes.

"Not today," I said. "Not now."

"We can talk on the phone," he said, holding out his hand. "And there's always e-mail."

"Yes." I moved to the bed and took the outstretched hand.

"You've been holding ice," he said.

"Against my face, so it wouldn't swell."

He brought his free hand up and covered his eyes.

"I can't take any more," he said.

"I know."

I waited until he could smile at me. Then I kissed him on the cheek and left.

At some point I was going to have to call Ramona. I would go up to the lake and take her to lunch. And I would have to talk to Sandra. Lane Josten and the TV people were on their own, even if I had to get Deke to threaten them again. At least they weren't congregating in front of my door.

In the meantime, I wanted to be alone in my cave.

I sat at my desk and ignored the phone until I realized the caller leaving a message was Deke.

"Just wanted to make certain we were on for dinner tonight," he said.

"Sure."

"Maybe I could even stop by early."

"No, don't do that. I'll see you at eight."

When it was time to leave, I realized I couldn't walk as far as the Mother Lode. And I was still cold enough to need my sheepskin jacket.

I parked the Jeep in the garage and walked across the alley.

The blast of noise and lights that hit me as I stepped through the air curtain was more discordant than usual. For the first time, the casino was an alien environment.

I took the escalator to the coffee shop.

Deke was waiting on his stool, sipping a cup of coffee.

"Somebody had to have called you." I settled uncomfortably on the adjacent stool. "Who was it this time?"

"Your friend Curtis. He felt he let you down, not making

you talk about whoever hit you in the head. And he hoped I could make up for it."

Deke waved at the Urrutia girl. I couldn't remember her name, but I smiled when she brought me a beer.

"Your head—" she began.

Deke cut her off with a frown.

She sort of bobbed at me and backed away.

"I don't think you can make up for it," I said, twisting the top off the beer.

"I think what he was hoping was that you would understand he wants to be around when all this is over, when both of you are healed."

"I don't know when that will be. And I'm not sure it will matter then, whether he wants to be around."

"Give it time. Right now I want to know about your head."

He knew some of it. The discovery of Cate's body had been on the news. The rest of it was fresh for him, fresh for me all over again as I told it.

"You didn't do anything wrong," he said when I was finished. "You did the best you could do. Better than most would have done."

"I guess so. I guess that's probably true." I wanted to feel it was true, but I was having trouble feeling. "And even if it is true, I still believe that something went terribly wrong, sometime, somewhere. Shooting people—killing people—isn't what I wanted to do, isn't what I set out to do when I decided to be a private investigator. God, I thought I wouldn't be much more than an errand runner, somebody who tracks down information that other people don't have the time and energy to track down for themselves."

"Life don't always turn out the way we think it will."

"Well, sure. But we have to have some kind of control over something about our lives. And I don't feel I've ever been in control of anything. For the last two and a half years, I've bounced from crisis to crisis, each one worse than the last. And that isn't what I want. A stone killer isn't who I want to be."

"It isn't who you are," Deke said. "No matter what happened last night."

"Last night was just the bottom of the bucket, when it hit me that the only choice I had was how I was going to die. I really believed that I could do one of three things with the single bullet in that gun—I could shoot Gonzales, I could shoot Danken, or I could shoot myself. And if I didn't use the bullet on myself, somebody else was going to shoot me." I tried the beer, but it didn't have much taste.

"Maybe that's all we can ever control, the way we die." Deke regarded me through red-rimmed eyes. "But I think you made some kind of statement about who you are, when you decided that your last act was going to be to take out the bad guy—the worst guy, they were all bad guys. You were willing to go out doing the only thing you could do that might leave life better for somebody else."

"Was I right?"

"I think so."

"You don't think I should have turned the gun on myself?"

"No. You weren't the worst guy. The bullet was for the worst guy."

"Maybe."

"And it left you alive. That's most important."

The Urrutia girl brought a steak and a hamburger and set them down in front of us, smiling brightly.

I wasn't sure I could eat. Deke thanked her and started in on his steak.

"It's time for something different," I said.

"You could have ordered chicken," Deke said around his mouthful.

"That's not what I mean." I picked up a French fry. "I

mean I have to do a better job with something. I don't know
what. But I know it's time for a change."

"Pass the ketchup," Deke said.

I passed him the mustard instead.